“So you admit that the

“Of course,” KC said, as if it m
circumstances.

Jacob stalked closer. “Why would you do this, KC? Was I really so horrible that you refused to let me be a part of—this?”

“That was never the issue, Jacob—”

“Then what was? Because I can’t imagine one big enough that you told yourself it was okay to deceive me. To keep my son a secret from me.”

Her arms crossed over her ribs, pushing those delectable breasts higher in the tank top. Something he shouldn’t notice right now. At all.

“I was afraid,” she said. “Going away just seemed the safest thing until I was sure what to do.”

“Safe? How? What the hell would safety have to do with it? I would never hurt you.”

“I know that, Jacob, but it wasn’t—”

“Fact is, you deprived me of three months of knowing my son,” he choked out. “Not a note, a card or a call. Hell, not even a text. *By the way, I’m pregnant*.”

He’d made himself available, chased after her like a dog with no sense, and *this* was what he got for it.

This time, he didn’t stop moving until he loomed over her petite frame. “So now, I’ll have what I want.”

* * *

The Blackstone Heir is part of the #1 bestselling series from Harlequin Desire, Billionaires and Babies—
Powerful men...wrapped around their babies’ little fingers.

* * *

If you’re on Twitter,
tell us what you think of Harlequin Desire!
#harlequindesire

Dear Reader,

This month, I invite you back to the town of Black Hills to once again witness the tragedies and triumphs of its ruling family, the Blackstones.

To me, there are few things more attractive than seeing a man learn to care for his child. I know this from years of experience—I fell in love with my husband all over again when each of our children was born! So I couldn't help but throw the all-business Jacob Blackstone into a situation where he had to prove he could learn to handle his secret son and the feisty blonde KC Gatlin.

I hope you enjoy the way she loosens his strictly professional persona and perfectly knotted tie, because I had so much fun throwing obstacles in his way.

As always, I love to hear from my readers. Please visit my website at daniwade.com or friend me on Facebook or Twitter!

Enjoy!

Dani Wade

THE BLACKSTONE HEIR

DANI WADE

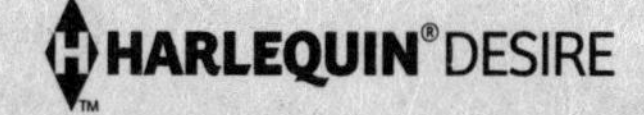

ISBN-13: 978-0-373-73368-2

The Blackstone Heir

This edition published by arrangement with Harlequin Books S.A.

For questions and comments about the quality of this book, please contact us at CustomerService@Harlequin.com.

Printed in U.S.A.

Dani Wade astonished her local librarians as a teenager when she carried home ten books every week—and actually read them all. Now she writes her own characters, who clamor for attention in the midst of the chaos that is her life. Residing in the southern United States with a husband, two kids, two dogs and one grumpy cat, she stays busy until she can closet herself away with her characters once more.

Books by Dani Wade

Harlequin Desire

His by Design

Milltown Millionaires Series

A Bride's Tangled Vows
The Blackstone Heir

Visit the Author Profile page
at Harlequin.com for more titles.

To Ms. Bobbie Tate—many years ago, you became my grandmother through marriage. You became my friend through your sweet spirit and my Maw Maw through your love. I can't thank you enough for being such a treasured part of my life.

One

"Hello, beautiful."

KC Gatlin heard the bell of a store door as she walked past on the sidewalk, but it simply registered as background noise. That voice, on the other hand, landed like a grenade on her senses. She could still hear the same words, the same deep sigh as she opened her door to him for the first time. Only this time he sounded not just sexy, but surprised.

Turning slowly, she found herself face-to-face with a man she had hoped not to see for many long, long months. The expectation was unrealistic, she knew, considering she once again lived in the same town as his family. The town he came home to visit often. His appearance now marked the approach of sure disaster, even as it brought into sharp focus how much she'd craved a glimpse of his tall runner's build and the unique blend of blonds in his close-cropped hair.

"Jacob Blackstone," she said, stalling while her brain struggled to come up with the flirty, easy responses for which she was known. They made her great tips as a waitress and bartender. But now, when she needed flippancy the most, it remained scarce. "What're you doing here?"

Stupid. There was a very logical reason why he would

be here: to check on his invalid mother, Lily Blackstone, now that his grandfather was dead and his brother Aiden had moved home. KC had just hoped to catch a few months' breather before facing her past.

Facing her mistakes.

"I mean, what are you doing on this end of town?" At least that question made sense. After all, Blackstone Manor was on the other side of Black Hills. But her fears, along with the steady, sober gaze of her former lover, had her brains whisked around like scrambled eggs. She had to get a handle on the panic jangling along her nerves.

He held up a small shopping bag. "Bandages. I needed to pick some up on my way home from work."

"Are you hurt—wait, home from work?" She tilted her head back for a better view of Jacob's face. She'd loved his height when they were together; how it sheltered her, protected her. Too bad that feeling of security had been nothing but an illusion.

"Yes, from the mill." He didn't look away, his gorgeous amber eyes with their unusual swirl of dark chocolate boring into her. She wanted a break from his unrelenting stare…and paradoxically wished she could bask in his attention. While her reactions ricocheted inside her, he went on, "I guess you haven't been home long enough to hear the news?" His voice rose at the end in a question, along with his brow.

"I guess not. I just moved back this week." Her stomach slowly turned over. Once. Then again. Why had her family not told her before she came home? The answer was obvious: they wanted her here, with them. She might never have returned if she'd known Jacob was now a permanent resident of Black Hills again.

She and Jacob had met on a plane to Black Hills—she'd been coming home from visiting her aunt in Seattle and had made a connecting flight in Philadelphia, where Jacob had been flying from to check on his mother. They'd seen each other every time he'd come to town since. Then reality had caught up with her in the threats of Jacob's grandfather and she'd gone to live with her aunt. A world away from this fascinating man and what they'd shared together.

She'd thought returning to her family would be safe now that James Blackstone was dead and gone. His threats to take away the livelihood of three single women unable to defend themselves—and a lifetime of proof that he'd do it—would finally be over. She'd known she would have to handle Jacob eventually, but had hoped to have more time. Much more.

She had a feeling he was about to burst her bubble.

"I've moved back to Black Hills to help Aiden run the mill. He has to split his time between here and New York, and with all the problems at the mill, we wanted a full-time presence."

"Yes, I heard that there were some odd things happening over there," she murmured. *Full-time?* The Lord must be punishing her for the secrets she kept.

Speaking of secrets... She tilted her head to the side as unobtrusively as possible to get a glimpse of the sidewalk behind Jacob. Her mother and grandmother were due to come out of the general store any minute. While she knew she had to talk to Jacob soon, she would prefer not to do it on the sidewalk in front of Parson's Pharmacy with the whole town looking on.

At least she had one thing going for her: Main Street was lined with miniature Bradford pear trees that would keep any busybodies from getting a clear view from the surrounding stores. In late spring, they were packed with white blooms that afforded even more privacy. Maybe no one would see more than just two neighbors greeting each other.

If she caused a scene on the sidewalk, Jacob would probably have a conniption. Months of him not taking her anywhere in public in Black Hills had taught her that much.

In the year they'd dated, Jacob had never introduced her to his family, never taken her *out* on a date. They'd spent evenings at her house, cooking, watching movies and making love before he went home to Philadelphia. She'd gone to visit his apartment there once, hoping to learn more about the city he loved enough to leave his family behind. Maybe a little about his work as the head of a large manufacturing company. But they'd never made it out of the apartment. KC had craved a real love all her life, after being abandoned over and over again as a child. Jacob wasn't looking for love… Still, she'd wanted him, so she'd forced herself not to need more from him.

His actions had made it obvious he wasn't interested in a long-term relationship, so she'd ignored her secret yearning for more. She'd been too afraid of losing him to insist. Responsiblc, steady guys usually didn't look at her twice—after all, she worked in a bar. But it wasn't just his incredible looks, smart, confident attitude or how good he'd been at rocking her world. Until she'd disappeared, Jacob had been attentive, caring and sexy—everything she'd ever wanted. But never committed—which was the one thing she'd needed him to be.

"Waiting for someone?" Jacob asked, folding his arms across his chest.

Oh, how she remembered that stance. He mostly resorted to it when he was disapproving or uncertain and didn't want anyone to know it. She'd jokingly called it his Dom stance, though Jacob didn't need power games to keep the bedroom interesting. His tightened muscles and locked legs exuded a commanding aura that sent shivers down her spine. Jake had strength in spades, but she hadn't trusted him to use it *for* her, to keep her. Her childhood had taught her it wouldn't happen.

She must have gotten lost in her thoughts, because Jacob bent closer, looming over her. "A new man, perhaps?"

A man? She'd thought she could be happily done with

the whole species for quite a while, until today. Jacob Blackstone had jump-started her tingling all over again. That intense gaze sent her heart racing and mouth watering. "Um, actually, my mom is on her way. Just checking for her, that's all."

Wow, this was so far from her usual easy conversations that she felt as if her secret was screaming from her guilty heart. Still, she could use his assumptions to her advantage.

"But yes, I do have a new man in my life." Jacob didn't need to know in what capacity after all. Anything to keep him at arm's length as long as possible.

"Is that why you changed your number…after refusing to answer your phone for weeks?"

Whoa. Not the direction she'd anticipated. But then, Jacob Blackstone had never failed to surprise her. There were whole areas of his life she knew absolutely nothing about.

"Look, Jacob, I'm really sorry. That was very bad of me." But she'd been carrying a heavy load with no idea what direction to go. A reason, not an excuse. She'd finally run far away, only returning once James Blackstone was dead. If she'd known Jacob would return, too—but no. Keeping secrets from him forever wasn't fair. She simply needed time. Time that was now draining away with the speed of sand in an hourglass.

"I just want to know why," he said, toned shoulder muscles flexing beneath his dress shirt. How did a CEO maintain such incredible physique…and stamina? She had to remind herself that it hadn't been enough, that she needed a man who would fight for her, no matter what anyone else thought.

"Did you think I couldn't handle the news that you wanted to break it off?" he asked.

"I…" Across the street, KC noticed a group of familiar women strolling down the sidewalk. Black Hills was a relatively small town. Everyone knew most everyone else.

Standing on Main Street talking with Jacob was the equivalent of standing on a stage. She needed to escape before someone started paying attention—

Or her mother and grandmother made an appearance.

"I just… Well, I didn't know how to tell you I wasn't interested anymore, actually." Clunky, but the truth. Knowing she'd chosen the cowardly way out, she still forced herself to sidestep him, then back away. "And you never seemed to want to deal with any deeper stuff, so…really, Jake, I'm just, well, sorry."

Then she turned and walked away, praying she could sidetrack her mother and grandmother before they proceeded to parade her baby down Main Street. She couldn't let Jacob learn about his son that way. Because he'd take one look and realize the main reason why she'd disappeared, if not the whole truth. As much as his arm's-length attitude had confused her, he didn't deserve that.

Which meant instead of the months she'd convinced herself she had to introduce Jacob to his son, she only had a matter of days. And she probably needed to figure out how to do that sooner rather than later.

Jacob Blackstone was too good at reading people not to realize when someone was lying. KC Gatlin showed all the signs.

This afternoon she'd shifted from side to side, avoided answering directly and refused to look him in the eye. Much to his deep disappointment.

He'd anticipated that moment when their eyes would meet more than anything. He was still thinking about it as he sat with his brothers in a booth directly opposite the bar at Lola's, sharing a platter of man food—wings and cheesy bacon-covered French fries—and alcohol. Jacob's drink of choice had always been wine. His brothers ragged him about his caviar tastes, but Jacob refused to apologize for having the most refined sensibilities of the family.

KC was far from refined. She'd been the burn of whiskey his body had been waiting for. That was why he'd ached for her to look at him this morning. He remembered well the sparks that would explode inside him just from sharing her gaze. His long-dormant body craved another taste, like a kid craved Pop Rocks.

He'd never forget their first meeting. From the moment she'd taken the plane seat next to him, he'd been enamored. That first conversation had revealed intelligence and humor in a beguiling mix. When they'd landed at the airport an hour away from Black Hills, he'd offered to share a ride. From that moment on, whenever he'd been in town, he'd spent as much time at her place as Blackstone Manor, until she'd stopped answering his phone calls months later. When he'd come home for his grandfather's funeral, she'd been nowhere to be found. The little house they'd spent so many enjoyable hours in had been sealed up tight.

He didn't want to, was shocked that he couldn't stop, but he'd hungered for her since that very first plane ride together. Time and distance hadn't changed that, much to his disgust. Nothing about his obsession made sense. They lived in two different worlds. They had two very different personalities and approaches to life. Still, he wasn't ready to let her go.

She'd been as wild as he'd expected, but she'd also led him to more genuine fun than he'd had his entire adult life. Quiet nights at home with a movie, cooking for two and sleeping in—oddities in his workaholic routine. No woman had interested him in any way beyond the physical. KC had interested him in every way.

She still did.

"Excuse me, guys."

Leaving his brothers staring after him, he made his way around tables to cross the room. They'd been in their corner for an hour while KC tended bar, and she hadn't looked directly at him a single time. Every second without that connection had itched below his skin until he couldn't even concentrate on the conversation. He'd deliberately kept their relationship out of the local headlines, but Jacob was desperate enough to risk a little limelight right now.

Oh, boy. His attitude made him very afraid he might step into stalker mode now that the possibility of seeing her around was very, very real. Some days, thoughts of KC had made him feel as if he was losing his mind.

He braced himself for her special brand of sarcasm. Something that had been noticeably lacking this morning.

"Jake. What brings you in tonight?"

You. Jacob ground his teeth together. Not because the shortening of his name bothered him, but because hearing it said in KC Gatlin's husky voice reminded him of evenings being soothed by her presence after an upsetting day with his mom. Reminded him of long nights between the sheets.

Far too distant memories.

"Do I need a reason? Can't I just enjoy the opportunity to watch a beautiful woman work the crowd?"

For the better part of a year, such a simple comment would have had her eyes sparkling, those full, naturally red lips tilting into a luscious smile, her mouth ready and willing to talk back. But not tonight.

"You never came to watch me before," she said, then dropped her gaze to the bar and started scrubbing, leaving him bereft once more. *So she wasn't gonna make this easy.*

He settled on a bar stool, watching that compact body displayed to advantage in a tight T-shirt and jeans. She acknowledged the move with a quick flick of her lashes, then studiously avoided looking at him again.

Just the way she'd ignored his phone calls. For seven months. He should have moved on by now, but his obsession had only grown. Now this successful, accomplished businessman found himself hunting the woman he craved in the local honky-tonk, because, well…because the cravings had become unbearable.

It no longer mattered that he couldn't figure out how she would fit into his life plan without wreaking havoc on it. She was the woman he shouldn't want, but the one woman he couldn't forget.

So he sucked up the little pride he had left and leaned closer. "You never did say where you'd been, KC."

She paused, then dropped the towel and met his gaze head-on. One of the things that had long enticed him was the very moment those turbulent hazel eyes turned his way, letting him see the woman inside and her mood, based on the dominant color of the day. Blue for calm and sunny. Green for sultry and sexy. Brown for angry or sad.

On tonight's menu: swirling milk chocolate. Wonder what he'd done to piss her off.

He'd never had a clue. They'd hooked up every time he'd come home to see his mother or take care of some business for his grandfather, until he'd found himself making up excuses just to return to Black Hills so he could see her. Watch her face while he talked with her. Sleep wrapped around her sweet-scented body. Hell, he'd even flown her out to Philadelphia once when he'd had to cancel his trip to Black Hills because of business.

Man, that had been a weekend to remember.

But the blank look on her face told him she wasn't into reminiscing. How much of a glutton for punishment was he willing to be?

"Come on, KC. Even as a friend, don't I deserve an answer?"

"I thought silence was my answer."

Burn. "Right."

For just a moment, the blankness slipped, revealing a flash of emotion that he couldn't interpret before it disappeared. But it revealed one important clue: indifference wasn't the problem.

So what was she hiding?

The KC he'd known had been all on the outside, open

with her emotions and actions. This closed-off version made him curious…and angry.

What had stripped away her joy, her spontaneity? Whatever it was, her attitude seemed to be reserved solely for him. He'd been watching her flirt and smile with other customers for an hour. The minute he'd appeared in front of her—shutdown.

Funny thing was, her spontaneity was one of the main things that drew him—and the one thing that had always kept him distant. Just thinking about living with uncertainty brought the barriers up. Other people found that kind of living by the seat of your pants exciting. He had enough of the unexpected in his life dealing with his twin; he didn't need more on a permanent basis. Luke's need for speed was as far from Jacob's scheduled existence as one could be from the other. Not to mention that his high-risk career as a race-car driver worried Jacob a lot.

So again he had to ask: Why was he sitting here instead of celebrating his freedom from his own version of risk?

"Was it because of this mystery man? Did you move to be with him?" Though the thought of her finding someone else hurt, maybe it was for the best. He needed something to break this incredible, horrible addiction.

She leaned closer, bracing against the bar. With her petite frame, the edge hit her higher than her waist, which gave him a really good view of her breasts in her tight Lola's T-shirt.

He was only human. Of course he looked.

Wait, was he seeing things? Because she seemed curvier than he remembered.

"Jacob," she said, drawing his gaze upward to her expectant face. Luckily she didn't call him on where he'd been looking. "Look, let's not do this here, okay? Another time, maybe."

"Why?" And why was he continuing to push this? "Is he here?"

"No, Jacob, that's not it."

The sudden sound of a phone ringing didn't register at first. After all, the bar was full of music, laughter and talking from the Friday-evening crowd. But the ringtone was persistent, and gained volume until he couldn't miss it. KC pulled out her phone and took one look at the display before answering.

She turned away, taking a few steps down the bar while she talked. He would have thought she'd completely dismissed him, except for the quick glances she kept shooting his way. After a few words he couldn't hear, she disconnected. Then she simply walked away.

His body mourned. His sensibilities raged. What did he have to do to get a simple explanation? Something more than "I'm sorry." Was that really too much to ask?

Determined to get answers, he stood up and strode after her. He came around the far side of the bar to catch a quick glimpse of her slipping out the back door. He knew her mother and grandmother lived in a small house behind the bar, so that must be where she was heading. If he intercepted her on her way back in, he could confront her without an audience.

All the better.

He could just make out her figure in the darkness as he made his way outside. Her body was silhouetted in the porch light from her family's house. He slowed his long stride. As she mounted the steps, the door opened and a woman who looked enough like her to be her mother stepped out.

That was when he heard another noise. But what caught his attention in that moment was what the older woman was holding.

A crying baby.

Jacob's world narrowed to the child.

"Goodness, girl." The voice of KC's mother drifted to

where he stood in the darkness. "I can't get Carter to stop crying for nothing. He wants his mama and no one else."

Jacob's legs carried him closer, his brain on hold as he tried to comprehend what he was seeing.

KC reached for the baby with the ease of a woman familiar with the move. The crying stopped almost immediately as she snuggled the child close into the crook of her neck. So natural. So beautiful.

So his.

The knowledge exploded over him in a wave of heat. As she swayed in the porch light, Jacob couldn't look away from the unusual dark golden curls that covered the baby's head.

"My brother and I had those same kind of curls," he murmured inanely.

In the newfound silence, they must have heard. KC jerked around to face him. But it was her mother Jacob found himself watching as the older woman's rounded eyes confirmed the suspicions in Jacob's whirling brain.

"KC," she said sharply, then stepped back through the door into the house.

KC didn't look in his direction again. She disappeared through the yellow rectangle of light in the entrance before slamming the door behind her, leaving Jacob alone in the dark.

It took a moment to get his feet to obey. As if by remote control, they carried him back to his brothers. He sank into the seat without really feeling it, seeing any of it. The numbness kept him from thinking, from dealing with the reality of what he'd just seen.

The bubble burst as he looked across the booth at his twin brother. Instantly, images of photographs from their childhood flooded his brain. Two boys, both with that thick dark blond hair. Curls all over until they'd gotten old enough to tame them.

"Jacob?" Luke said, hunching forward into his line of vision. "Jacob, are you okay? Where'd you go?"

Reaching out, Jacob picked up his half-full glass of wine and lifted it to his lips to perform the ultimate wine drinker's depravity. He chugged until every single drop was gone.

Then he set the glass down carefully and lay his palm flat beside it, praying the solidity of the table would ground him in the spinning room.

Luke lay his own palm on the table, mirroring Jacob's. "You cool?" Their version of letting each other know they were there.

And just like that, the words came to him, along with the anger. "I think I'm a daddy."

Two

Twenty-four hours later, Jacob finally stopped seething enough to confront KC. When he'd imagined what it would be like to find out he was going to be a parent, he'd pictured being across the table from his wife at an intimate dinner or seated next to each other in a doctor's office. Instead, the most gorgeous woman in the world had made him a father—and failed to mention it for twelve months.

The numbness had melted into rage, keeping Jacob awake long into the night. He went over the figures time and again. They hadn't spoken for seven months—he was ashamed that he could remember it to the day. He didn't have a lot of experience, but he'd guess the baby to be three to four months old. So how long had she known she was pregnant before she left? Two months? Three? Either way, they'd definitely been together when she found out. And those curls proved the baby to be a Blackstone heir.

He knew better than to see her before he calmed down. He couldn't be responsible for his actions while struggling with the deepest emotions he'd ever known. Control was his drug of choice—being out of control was something he preferred to keep well hidden. So he waited until he had his reactions under lock and key, and then he got in the car and drove.

KC lived a little outside town in a tiny house. Though there were other houses around, it wasn't really a subdivision. More of a series of dwellings that had sprung up over time as family members and friends and even acquaintances bought land and started building. The result was individual, with plenty of space and large trees. Ideal starter homes. Just imagining the possibilities ignited his anger once more.

He knew she'd be there—familiarity with her schedule gave him an advantage.

Sure enough, the door opened before he even knocked. She didn't speak, but simply turned back into the house, leaving him to follow. His gaze tracked her, cataloging every inch as she walked to the far end of the living room. Yeah, that body had changed, all right.

If he'd known what he was looking for, he'd have noticed right away. He'd been too busy searching for a connection in her eyes. But drinking in the whole package in jeans and a tank top, he saw the more dramatic curve from her waist to her hips, the added fullness in her breasts and a touch of softness in her jawline.

He'd thought nothing could make her more beautiful, but somehow having his baby had. And he hadn't been allowed to be a part of it.

Irritation with his attraction only ramped up his intensity. Carefully shuttering every window to his soul, he faced off with her in true Blackstone fashion.

He jerked his head in the direction of the driveway. "Someone else here?" he asked, referring to the car parked behind hers. So help him, if there was a man living here, he just might explode. Had she moved on that quickly? Had she let another man care for Jacob's child?

"Mom," she said quietly, slightly dampening his fuse. "She's in the nursery with Carter."

His throat almost closed. "Carter, huh?"

"Yes. Jake Carter."

Jake. Her nickname for Jacob—spoken with laughter, with intensity, with passion. It seemed more personal to name the baby that than to give him Jacob's last name.

"So you admit that he's mine?"

"Of course," she said, as if it made perfect sense under the circumstances. How could anything she'd done make perfect sense?

He stalked closer. "Why would you do this, KC? Was I really so horrible to you that you refused to let me be a part of—this?"

"That was never the issue, Jacob—"

"Then what was?" A really deep breath helped him lower his voice. It kept rising without his permission. *Control.* He needed control. "What *was* the issue, KC? Because I can't imagine one big enough that you told yourself it was okay to deceive me. To keep my son a secret from me."

Her arms crossed over her ribs, pushing those delectable breasts higher in the tank top. Something he shouldn't notice right now. At all.

"I did not deceive you. I never lied. I was going to tell you. I just hadn't figured out how."

"So he's three months old?"

"Yes, a week ago."

"So at any time in the past twelve months you could have picked up the phone. Or hell, just answered the phone when I called."

"I was afraid to. Going away just seemed the safest thing until I was sure what to do."

Jacob was surprised by the low rumble of his voice. "Safe? How? What the hell would safety have to do with it? I would never hurt you."

"I know that, Jacob, but it wasn't—"

The emotional roller coaster of the night caught up with him, pushing him past reasonable thought. "Know what?

It doesn't matter. Fact is, you deprived me of three months of knowing my—son," he choked out. "Not a note, a card or a call. Hell, not even a text. *By the way, I'm pregnant.* That's all it would have taken, KC, but you didn't even have the decency to do that."

He'd made himself available, chased after her like a dog with no sense, and *this* was what he got for it.

He came even closer until he loomed over her petite frame. "So now, I'll have what I want."

He wished her deep breath didn't draw his gaze downward. The low-level buzz of desire beneath his anger made him want to curse. He should not be attracted to a woman who could betray him. But he couldn't help it.

"Jake, please let me explain."

He refused to look in those turbulent eyes again. "Too late. No talking. No thinking. Now I will act."

She straightened, bracing her spine, which was just as well.

"Carter will come home."

Her jaw clenched. "He is home."

"My home." Some sick part of him took pleasure in the panic creeping over her features. "He's a Blackstone. He should be with his family."

She swallowed hard. "Jacob, please don't do this."

"Mark my words, KC. I will make you regret what you've done. I promise."

As soon as he'd stormed out of her house, KC began to dread the moment Jacob would act on his threat. The longer she waited, the more her stomach hurt.

She knew she'd made a bad choice, but given the circumstances, she thought she'd done the best she could. Waiting until James Blackstone was dead to tell Jacob about Carter had seemed like the safest option for protecting her baby, along with her family. In the absence of a reliable husband or father, her mother had given her all to raising and providing for KC and her brother. KC had felt that pull of loyalties every day that she'd been away, but in the end, she'd chosen to take care of the women who had raised her. Her mother and grandmother would have no defense against James Blackstone if he'd retaliated by taking away their livelihood on a whim.

But Jacob didn't believe her, because he was acting on emotion, not facts.

How did she get him to listen to those facts now? She knew James's lawyer, Canton, could work all kinds of voodoo if he wanted. Was Jacob even now making arrangements to take her baby from her? The thought shook her deeper than any of the rest. Not just for the typical mommy reason: being away from her child for more than a day was more than she could handle right now. But Jacob was essentially an unknown as a parent.

Would he expose their child to the same rejection and abandonment she'd been subjected to as a child? In her experience, fathers didn't know the meaning of commitment. But she'd been luckier than her brother. Her father had hung around until she was eight. Her older brother had never really known his.

After stewing for the rest of the morning, she decided she couldn't wait for Jacob to make the first move. Jacob wasn't answering his cell, which scared her all the more. When she called Blackstone Manor directly, the old butler answered. She'd spoken to Nolen a few times before when she'd called to talk to her friend Christina, who'd married Jacob's brother. Nolen was helpful, telling her that Jacob had said something about going to Booties 'n' Bunting.

Panic and anger had surged in KC's gut. Booties 'n' Bunting was the only exclusive baby boutique in town. Jacob had the money to do all the things she couldn't. She'd bought all her baby furniture and clothes at Walmart. He'd have designer diapers and the best furniture, not to mention the best lawyer when it came down to a fight.

She'd made the mistake; now it was up to her to ensure that it didn't turn into a brawl.

KC's stomach twisted into knots as she drove across Black Hills. Whipping her little Honda into Booties 'n' Bunting's parking lot, she jumped out of the car and plowed down the sidewalk, not letting herself remember just how little she belonged in the boutique district, much less in a store selling fifty-dollar baby onesies. Jacob's Tahoe parked out front confirmed that he was here. No doubt arming himself with everything he needed to take her child away.

She let herself in with her head held high and tracked down her prey, standing next to the most gorgeous crib she'd ever seen.

"What do you think you're doing?"

Jacob faced her with surprise lightening his face. For a split second, KC saw the man she'd wanted more than anything. Then a mocking grin slid across his lips.

"Could you give us a minute, please?" Jacob asked the saleswoman. Until that moment, KC hadn't even noticed her on the other side of the crib. The woman turned quietly and walked to the back of the store before Jacob continued, "What does it look like, KC? I'm outfitting the nursery at Blackstone Manor."

Oh, no, he wasn't. "You don't need any of this stuff, Jacob, because Carter is *not* coming to live with you."

"And what makes you say that?"

"This isn't just about you, Jake. You need to think about what's best for Carter."

"I am. I have the means to provide my son with everything he needs. Unlike you."

Hurt streaked through her, but she pushed it deep down under her growing anger. "Really? Can you give him love? Can you comfort him? Can you guide him? Or are you planning on using your money to turn that job over to a nanny so you can go about your perfectly planned days?"

His narrowed eyes should have had her shaking, but

she refused to back down. Her son's future was at stake. She didn't want to hurt Jacob, but how else could she get through to him? "One thing I can say with certainty is that I can provide him those things. You, I'm not so sure about."

Not waiting to give him a chance to outthink her, she pushed forward. Crowding into Jacob's space, she said, "You want Carter to come live with you? I understand why you would. I don't blame you for that." Her breath caught for a moment. "And I don't blame you for not trusting me, but I'm not turning my son over to just anyone."

"Oh, you don't have to turn him over," Jacob said, his voice deepening as if he had gravel in his throat. "You can come, too. I'm sure I could find a…use…for you."

Strike number two. How many body shots did he plan to take? Because she sure didn't need the reminder that Jacob had wanted her for sex and only sex.

She wasn't sure how long she stood there with wide eyes before he looked away. But he wasn't backing down. "The fact is, you've had Carter to yourself for three months. Your time just ran out."

She'd guessed Jacob was a formidable businessman. But when he turned that laser-sharp stare on her, it sliced through what little armor she had and put every inner doubt on display.

"Jacob, I understand your anger," she said, trying to slow her panic with a deep breath. "I made a horrible miscalculation. So I want to do my part to make this work. But no lawyers. No fighting. You want Carter to be a part of your life? Prove it to me." *Please, please, let this work.*

"What do I need to prove? We knew each other for over a year. You know everything you need to know about me."

"I know everything about certain parts of you." If he wanted the truth, she could comply. "I know you're halfway decent in bed." That whopper of an understatement almost choked her. "How good you are at picking up girls on planes. That you enjoy being with me at home but don't want to be seen in public with me. That I'm good enough for sex but not allowed into any other part of your life. None of that tells me a damn thing about what kind of father you are."

"So you want me to prove I can change diapers?" His shocked expression would be a thing to savor later when she stopped being so afraid of him that she might wet her pants.

"I want to know that you're more than a sexual being, Jacob. Show me what kind of man you truly are. Can I trust your word? Can I believe you when you say you aren't bad-mouthing me to my child behind my back? Can I trust you to teach him morals and work ethic and decency? Because I won't let *my child* become a chip off James Blackstone's block."

Jacob stepped closer, literally towering over her. "What the hell are you talking about?"

Arching her neck to stare at him wasn't comfortable, but she wasn't going to concede with even a single step backward. "Since you didn't know about Carter, I'm going to guess and say you didn't know your grandfather came to see me right before he died."

"Aiden would have told me."

"Did Aiden know? He wasn't there."

"Who was?"

"That lawyer guy."

"Canton?"

"That's the one. They came to the house one morning. I'd only known I was pregnant for a week."

"How could he possibly know about that?"

KC shook her head. "I'm not sure. But he did know how long we'd been seeing each other. I wouldn't put it past either of them to spy on me somehow."

Jacob's Adam's apple shifted in his throat. KC was sorry to have to deliver her news.

"James knew you were pregnant with my child." The deadness in his voice reverberated through her. She'd often wondered how a man like his grandfather could have had a child. What kind of family did you create with manipulation and fear? No wonder Aiden Blackstone had run far, far away when he was younger.

Though Jacob had always seemed quite normal, she'd sensed a dark sadness underneath that excellent control of his. What games had James Blackstone played with his grandsons? What terror had he wreaked in their family before he died? Jacob had never even come close to sharing something that personal.

"That's the only reason I could think of that he would demand I leave town. And never come back."

Jacob seemed frozen; not a muscle moved. He gripped the crib rail with one hand. The knuckles turned white… and stayed white.

"But you didn't stay away."

"No. Once I found out he was dead, I thought the coast would be clear to come home." That might have been a mistake, too. "But he threatened my family's business—"

"How?" he asked, his eyes narrowing as if he suspected a lie.

"Jacob," she said, shaking her head at him, "your grandfather owned half the town. He'd rented us the land Lola's is on for my entire life but never would allow my mother or grandmother to buy it. I suspect it was so he could use it to his advantage if the opportunity arose."

She tried to breathe around the anger that rose at the memory. "He threatened to shut down the business. Everything my mother and grandmother own is tied up in Lola's. Not to mention that their house is on that land, too. So I agreed, and the men left. Then I cashed out some savings and used it to move away."

Jacob smirked. "Serves him right."

"When I heard about his death, I thought—well, we all thought—he couldn't hurt us anymore. I just hadn't figured out what to do about you yet."

"And you think this is the answer?"

"It's the only one I've got." Might as well be honest about that. "Let's face it, Jacob. You have money and a damn good lawyer. But James didn't own me, and neither do you. If you want to be part of Carter's life, stop throwing your weight around and work with me."

"Who put you in charge? You haven't exactly proved yourself trustworthy."

Unease rippled through her body. She knew she'd had good reasons for her choices, but when she looked at it from his point of view… "I'm not denying you access to Carter out of anger or revenge, Jacob. I simply want to know that he's in good hands. That you're willing to make a place for a baby in your life. Not hand him over to a well-paid nanny."

His eyes searched hers. "How can I be sure he's in good hands with you?"

"I— Well—" Words failed her for a moment.

"Face it, KC. You ran halfway across the country to hide my child from me. I'm not the only one with something to prove. The question is, how?"

Three

Jacob hadn't felt so out of control since the last time he'd had KC in a bed. Only, anger wasn't nearly as pleasurable. Still, he used the impetus to propel himself through the door to his brother Aiden's study at Blackstone Manor, knowing John Canton was there for a meeting.

This morning, Aiden had mentioned an appointment for the lawyer to drop off some paperwork for their grandfather's will. Canton still had control of the Blackstone inheritance, for now. There were some final hoops to jump through, then Jacob and his brothers would be free of James Blackstone and his minion.

"You bastard," Jacob growled, absorbing his brother's shocked look as he passed. But his focus was trained wholly on the lawyer.

The same lawyer who had assisted their grandfather in blackmailing Aiden into marrying Christina, their mother's nurse, terrorizing them with threats of compromising their mother's health and care if they didn't comply.

"I knew you would force two people to get married to suit James's purposes. Threaten, and bully, and even ruin an entire town on the whim of a dead man. But I seriously thought any decent human being would draw the line at cutting a child completely out of a man's life." He let his momentum carry him until he loomed over the smaller man. "Guess I thought wrong."

From behind the desk, Aiden asked, "Jacob, care to fill me in?"

Canton didn't even blink…or pretend not to understand what Jacob referred to. "I did as your grandfather ordered."

"Didn't you think I should have a say?"

Canton shrugged. "That was not for me to decide."

With a growl, Jacob reached forward, but arms made of steel were there to stop him. Slowly, Aiden inched him back until there was enough room for him to stand between Jacob and the man he felt like killing.

"I've obviously missed something," Aiden said. "Tell me now."

From the other side of the barrier Aiden provided, Canton spoke. *Brave man.* "I believe Jacob is referring to a conversation his grandfather had with Ms. Gatlin."

"What?" Aiden looked surprised.

Jacob turned away, relieving his brother of guard duty. At least not looking at his grandfather's lawyer would help him regain control. In thirty-three years, he'd never experienced this many emotional twists. He didn't like it. He needed stability. All the more reason to stay away from KC—but that wasn't an option anymore.

He turned back, focusing on his brother. "I went to see KC Gatlin."

Aiden gave a short nod. "So it's true? The baby is yours?"

"He's three months old." Jacob felt the need to clarify, now that he had more facts. "I met KC on one of my flights home and…" How did he put this without making it sound as if KC was simply a booty call? "Okay, I was sleeping at her place whenever I came to town." Why sugarcoat his selfishness?

Aiden's thick brows went up. "Wow, Jacob. I didn't know you had it in you."

"Not the time, Aiden."

"Really? You brought it up."

Jacob ignored the brotherly razzing and moved on. "The baby is definitely mine." That shut down his brother's grin. Real quick. "Dear ol' Grandpa threatened her until she skipped town, never telling me about it—my son."

Aiden narrowed his gaze on the lawyer. "How would Grandfather even find out KC was pregnant? Medical records are confidential. Was he rummaging through her trash for a pregnancy test?"

Jacob barely held his control as he waited for the answer.

Canton smirked. "Anything can be had for the right price. Turns out, one of the little nurses at KC's doctor has a serious cash-flow problem."

Jacob was rushing forward before he even thought. Only the barricade created by Aiden's body stopped his attack. His own heavy breathing sounded loud in Jacob's ears; his heart thudded as he realized the full magnitude of his grandfather's invasion of privacy. Jacob wanted to do bodily harm all over again.

"Easy," Aiden murmured against his ear. "Let's get our questions answered, and then he'll be gone. Forever this time."

Silence reigned as Jacob tried to gather the remnants of his self-control. His thoughts whirled, reminding him if he hadn't come home for good, he might never have found out he was a father. Pulling back, he announced, "It was only by accident I found out that KC had my child."

Canton spoke again from a safe distance across the room. "Then I don't understand the issue."

Jacob rounded on him but didn't move closer. He didn't trust himself. "The issue? You tried to separate me from my child."

"But by your own admission, we didn't succeed."

The guy simply didn't get it. "Would you ever have told me?"

"Your grandfather demanded complete loyalty. And discretion. Of course I wouldn't have." His weasel-like face didn't change expression. "And since Ms. Gatlin moved without contacting you and didn't come home during the remainder of your grandfather's lifetime, she'd fulfilled our terms. In which case, there was nothing to tell."

"I'm glad you think so. I guess that clears your conscience."

The man didn't bother to defend himself. "I don't have a conscience. I have a job."

"That's enough," Aiden interjected. "Canton, we're done for now. I'll reschedule with you *at your office* later and we will finish up the last of the paperwork for Grandfather's affairs."

The lawyer was smart enough to take an out when it was given to him. He scurried through the door without so much as a by-your-leave. But his departure ratcheted down Jacob's anger by a few notches.

"Man, I'll be glad to see the last of that guy," Aiden said as he straightened the papers on his desk.

"How much longer?"

Aiden had spent the year dealing with his grandfather's lawyer after James had blackmailed him into marrying Christina. Luckily, it had all worked out for the best, but the lawyer's presence was an annoying reminder of their grandfather's manipulations.

Aiden waved the papers at him. "This is the end of it. The year is almost up and we will be free from it all. Including Canton. I just wish there was a way to punish him for what he's done rather than be rewarded with the money Grandfather left him." Aiden settled back into his chair, looking every inch the sophisticated Manhattan art dealer, though he now lived in South Carolina instead of New York. "KC Gatlin, huh? Beautiful, but definitely different from your standard of socialites and fellow businesswomen."

"Tell me about it." Jacob started to pace, hoping to expend the energy thrumming beneath his skin. Hell, he just might have to go for another jog, even though he'd done five miles this morning. Especially as he thought about KC's earlier accusations.

"Where do you want to go from here?" Aiden asked after several moments.

More of that loaded silence.

Finally, Jacob said, "I would be lying if I said I didn't want to see her again. Didn't wish we could pick up where we left off when she disappeared. But—no." He glanced over at his brother. "She's not right for me long-term."

"Why not?"

Good question. "Let's see. She doesn't fit in with what I want in life, who I am. She's more like Luke—unpredictable, headstrong." *And makes me feel just as unpredictable. Out of control.*

"She's gorgeous."

"She works in a bar."

"Ah, a hard worker."

Jacob stared hard at the bookshelves, cataloging the shapes and colors of the books but not the titles. "She kept my son a secret."

"So she panicked and made a mistake. You enjoyed being with her before. What's the real problem?"

Could he let his guard down? Even a little? Jacob was used to his brothers confiding in him, not the other way around. "I just— Before, it was easy. But she's right. I kept her compartmentalized so I wouldn't have any interference in my life." He ran his hand across his close-cropped hair. "It had nothing to do with only wanting her for sex and everything to do with making our relationship convenient for me."

"Relationships are anything but convenient. I'm learning to roll with it because the good far outweighs everything else."

Jacob felt a moment of envy. Inflexibility seemed to have been bred into him. Strict adherence to standards and procedures served him well in business, not so much in relationships. At least, the few he'd had. He rarely saw a woman more than a handful of times, since he wasn't ready for the long-term thing yet. Maybe not for several more years.

KC had taken him off guard. He could admit to himself that he'd kept her compartmentalized in his life because he'd been afraid—afraid of her taking over, afraid of losing control, afraid of being ruled by emotions instead of his brain.

I want another chance at that woman. No. "She's my son's mother. Better to stay close and know your enemy, right?"

Aiden's smirk took him by surprise. "Jacob, the last time I fell for that line, I ended up married to the woman who changed my life, my way of thinking, forever. For the better, but still…"

"Not me."

Aiden's expression screamed *famous last words*, but Jacob ignored it. Aiden had vowed at eighteen never to return to Blackstone Manor—now he was happily married and living here full-time, with frequent business trips to New York to manage his art import/export business.

Would Jacob end up the same? Moving home was definitely the right choice, especially since his son was now here. But married? Not to KC. As exciting as being with her was, he wanted peace, not unpredictability.

"Jacob."

The serious tone in Aiden's voice cut through Jacob's confusion. "Yeah?"

"What are you going to do about KC? About the baby?"

"Carter," he said, clearing his throat when it tried to

close. "Forcing her to give him to me would probably lead to a legal battle—and prove me to be a jackass. She might not have a lot of money, but she won't give him up without a fight." He frowned. "The bigger question is, what is she gonna do about me?"

Aiden thought for a moment. "Do you want her?"

"I do, but I told you, she's not right—"

"Sometimes things don't come the way we plan."

And Jacob had been planning his entire life. He didn't know if he could give that up.

"I can't walk away. He's my son." Deep down he cringed at the hypocrisy of speaking as if memories of those incredible nights together had no influence on Jacob's desire to see KC again.

"Then you need to be very careful…for you and for them."

Jacob glanced over. "What do you mean?"

"I mean what's going on at the mill. We still haven't figured out who's trying to sabotage our business, and until we do, nobody associated with us is safe. Delaying shipments and messing with customers' orders is annoying, but what happened to Christina last year could have killed her. She wasn't the target, but that doesn't change the result."

Jacob remembered all too well the night a group of thugs had set Aiden's studio on fire…with Christina inside. The incident was one of many suspicious events at the Blackstones' cotton mill, but it had escalated the game to a whole new level. "You think they might target my son?"

"Not on purpose, but then again…" Aiden leveled a look at him, sending unease running over Jacob's nerve endings. "It would be for the best to keep the connection quiet. For now."

"Right." *For now.* Jacob had a lot of experience keeping things quiet in this town.

"So get control, before someone else does."

Like KC. Jacob had been irritated and fascinated at the

baby store. Until she'd burst in and started making demands, he hadn't known what it would be like to have all that feistiness turned on him as a weapon. His whole body had lit up inside. At this rate, she'd have the upper hand in no time. Leading him about by the nose, or rather, another appendage he'd just as soon keep under control.

Jacob was grateful when Aiden moved on, pulling him back out of his convoluted thoughts.

"Back to business," Aiden said. "I had a call from Bateman at the mill right before Canton arrived."

Jacob had had a call, too, but he'd let it go to voice mail. He'd been too keyed up from his clash with KC to make sense of business.

A problem he never had.

Deflating like a balloon, Jacob dropped into one of the chairs facing the desk, grateful Aiden had replaced the old leather-and-wood chairs with cozy wing backs. His brother and sister-in-law were slowly updating things in Blackstone Manor—especially the study—inch by inch scraping away the depressive stench of their grandfather's manipulation to reveal the true beauty of a home that had stood for generations in the face of natural and man-made tribulations.

"I just don't know how to get a handle on the problems at the mill," Jacob said, reminding them both of the year they'd spent dealing with the saboteur. "We need to find another way of catching this guy. I mean, I'm there every day, but I'm in management. And no one's talking to me. We need someone on the floor, someone relatable. I think that's where the problem is."

"Definitely can't be either of us. See if Bateman can put you in touch with someone over there to help. He'll know who's trustworthy."

"Right." His foreman had already been very helpful. Because Jacob wasn't capable of judging anyone at the moment. Business would give him something to focus on besides KC, just as soon as they settled on some ground rules.

Start as you mean to go on, his mother had always said. For everyone involved, that was exactly what they needed to do.

As she faced off with Jake on her front porch, KC knew she was simply delaying the inevitable, but she couldn't stop herself from arguing just for the sake of it. "What if my mom wasn't here to watch Carter?"

KC spoke with no real hope of making a dent in Jacob's thinking but couldn't resist pointing out the inconvenience he was putting everyone through. Everyone but him. She hated the push-pull of her emotions. Wanting to keep him at arm's length, yet greedy for even a little bit of his attention. When he'd finally called after two days of silence, her heart had sped up, but she couldn't help being contrary about his sudden demand for her to take a Sunday drive with him.

"If we're going to do this, there will be ground rules," he said now as he waited impatiently on her doorstep. "That means we need to talk. Alone."

That take-charge tone shouldn't send shivers down her arms but it did. "Yes, we should," she conceded. "But you still could've given me a heads-up sooner."

She took her time walking back to the nursery. Not that she had anything important to do on Sunday mornings. Her mother usually came over before lunch for some downtime with Carter since Lola's wasn't open. Sometimes KC ran a few errands. Then they had family dinner with Grandma. Asking her mother to stay with Carter for a little while was really a formality, but it also wouldn't hurt Jacob to wait on her porch a few minutes, just for giggles and grins.

Her pokiness had her changing into jeans and pulling her hair into a ponytail, but she simply refused to hurry. He didn't comment when she finally came outside, just held the door for her to climb into his Tahoe and closed it with a firm hand.

The contained atmosphere of Jacob's SUV didn't settle her nerves. The interior smelled like him—spicy and dark. If she closed her eyes and breathed deep, she could almost remember what it felt like to have that scent all over her and wish she didn't ever have to wash it away. After all, she never knew when she might smell it again.

After she'd left, been away from him for a while, she realized how sad it was to need someone so badly and yet be relegated mostly to a physical relationship. They said men did it all the time—obviously Jake had—but KC had never felt more alone than when she was lying in his arms, wishing she was good enough for him to make her a true part of his life.

The door opened and Jacob slid into his seat with his phone pressed to his ear. "I'm on my way," he said as he reached for his seat belt. Without explanation he stowed the phone in the center console. Then he put the Tahoe in gear and pulled out of KC's driveway, all without telling her where they were going or what this was about.

"You said something about ground rules?" she prompted.

Jacob maintained a still silence for several minutes more, at odds with the hum of the tires on asphalt. "I've made it clear what I want—"

"Actually, you haven't."

He shot a glance at her.

"Well, you haven't," she insisted. "Are you trying to get Carter full-time? Not that I'd let you have custody, but still…do you want him part-time? Have you thought about how that will work, how it will affect him? Do you—?"

"Enough, KC."

His deep frown had her second-guessing her pushiness, but she wouldn't apologize for trying to protect her son.

"I started making demands because I was angry. Unlike you, I didn't get to think about this, plan for this, nothing. So I reacted out of emotion." The heavy sound of his breath was her clue to how much self-control he was exerting.

A part of her, the wounded part, wanted to push him. Make him acknowledge that she and Carter would have a big place in his life—something he hadn't found important enough to offer her before. Another part of her wanted to see that legendary control smashed to teeny-tiny pieces.

Just the way it had when they were in bed together. But as soon as the sex had been done, he'd been back in form—charming and attentive but perfectly capable of walking away.

"We have to do what's best for Carter," he said, staring straight out the windshield. "So how do we do that?"

"Let me get to know you."

"To what end? What are we striving for here, KC?" He ran a rough hand over his smooth chin. In the time she'd known him, she'd never once seen him with stubble. "Because if you think you can disappear with him if you don't like what you learn, that's not an option. I will always find you."

But for all the wrong reasons. "My family is here, Jacob," she countered. "It didn't take me long to realize that running is not a safe, long-term option. I made a mistake—one I won't repeat. But I'd better like what I see, because unlimited access to your son *is* on the line." She shifted against the leather seat, wondering if she could back up her big words with action.

"Look," she said. "I don't want us to spend our time trying to guard against each other. If this is truly about Carter—" she ignored Jake's look "—then we need to work together. I tried to do things your way before and got nowhere. So this really is all on you. Show me what you're like out of bed so I can see where Carter and—" *I.* Carter and I. She cleared her throat, grateful she hadn't finished that sentence out loud. "Where Carter fits. Prove to me that he's in good hands with you."

"So what is it I'm supposed to do to show you I'm a

good man? Hell, even I don't know if I'm a good father. I've never been one before. Is this a written exam? A field test?"

"Oh, it's a field test, all right. No more secrets, Jacob."

He shot her a quick glance. "Are you seriously saying you didn't learn anything about me in the months we were together? Why don't you tell me what you do know and I'll fill in the blanks."

All the memories of their time together flooded her mind—long nights, laughter and loving… No. Not loving. The thought created an urge to get under his skin in the only way she knew how.

She shifted as close to him as her seat belt would allow. "Well," she said, reaching out a fingertip. "I know you're sensitive here." She brushed gently back and forth along the outer edge of his ear, then down along his jawline. "I know you shave early and often because you don't like looking scruffy." The back of her hand rubbed down along his throat, then up along his collarbone. "I know your favorite sexual position is missionary because it gives you the most control—"

"What do you want to know?" Jacob interrupted, his voice deep and rough.

She leaned back in her seat, trying to cover her smile of satisfaction. Torturing him had always been fun. "What do you do—I mean, really do? What do you care about? Enjoy? Do you plan on staying here for longer than just the time it takes to get the mill on track?"

"What about you?" he asked, countering a question with a question.

"What do you mean?"

"The same questions apply to you," he said, turning the Tahoe into a nearby parking lot so he could face her. "This won't be a one-way street, KC."

Yes, her sins would haunt her forever. She should never have kept Carter from Jake.

His gaze held her immobile as he spoke. "I'm not the

only one paying for my mistakes," he said, leaning closer, crowding her until her heart fluttered in panic. "We're gonna be seeing a lot of each other."

"I'm sure," she said with a nod, trying to get a handle on her nerves.

His gaze dropped to her lips as she licked them, reminding her of things she was better off forgetting. The space around them closed in before he spoke. "The thing is, with your history, I'm now questioning every word from these pretty lips."

She had no warning when his thumb came up to rub back and forth across her mouth. It affected her more than she wanted to admit, and left her dreaming of more.

"Consequences, KC. Those are *my* terms."

Her lips firmed, and she had a feeling she'd adopted the stubborn look she was known to turn on disruptive customers. Jacob simply smiled, then pulled back and got them on the road again.

"Well," she said, a little stumped, "my life is pretty simple, as you saw before. My job, my time revolves around my family."

"They're supportive? Of you and Carter?"

Her heart jumped at the softening of his voice as he said their son's name. "Definitely. Our family is very close. And my grandmother, mother and brother love Carter unconditionally."

Even if their new connection to the Blackstone family scared her mother no end. KC rubbed her palms against her jean-covered thighs, searching for more words. "What about your family?" She swallowed hard, distracted by thoughts of her friend Christina, a true Blackstone now. She would be so mad when she realized KC had kept the truth about Carter from her. "Did you tell them?"

"I guess you'll see," Jacob said, then turned the truck abruptly into a construction area.

With a start, KC realized they were at the site of the new

playground Aiden Blackstone had raised money to build on the south end of town. The large field had been cleared and leveled, with concrete slabs laid in various areas to anchor the equipment. Current construction seemed to center around a two-story fort at the far end.

There, a group of people stood to one side while a handful of construction workers drilled to secure the platforms. "Do they know we're coming?" she asked.

"They knew I was coming," Jacob said. "You'll just be the bonus."

Yeah, right.

Jacob settled his palm on the door's handle, then spoke while staring straight ahead. "And for the record, my favorite position isn't missionary. It's you on top."

KC swallowed hard. That revelation held her in place for longer than she liked. Her mind wandered back to all the times—no. No time for that now.

She'd be better off remembering all the times he'd left her to go back to Philadelphia with rarely a call between trips. KC scrambled out of the car, ignoring Jacob's frown. He'd always liked to open the door for her, and she'd trained herself to wait for him. It had been hard for a girl who'd always taken care of herself, but she'd done it because it made him happy. And deep down, because it made her feel special. Letting him do it now would be too big of a reminder of those precious moments.

As she followed at a slight distance behind him across the open lot, KC wished there was at least one happy face in the crowd. She recognized the newlywed couple as they approached, and neither looked very welcoming.

Yep, the news of Carter's parentage had spread.

Jacob introduced her to his brother, but Christina stepped in before he could go further. "We know each other," she said quietly. "Hey, KC."

KC couldn't read her friend's tone or expression. They'd been very close before KC left, often hanging out in the same group of women. But she, Christina and their friend Avery Prescott had formed a tight bond through community work that hadn't been weakened by their different social statuses. KC had told them she was moving away for a job, and other than some chance encounters, she hadn't tried to renew her bond with the women since she'd returned.

All it would have taken was one of them to figure out who Carter's father was, and they all would have known. Living and working in Blackstone Manor—and now married to the Blackstone heir—Christina posed a danger to KC. She hadn't wanted to risk anything until she had all her ducks in a row.

Seeing Christina now reminded KC how much she'd given up in the past year, but keeping Carter safe had been worth it.

"KC, I'm sorry we've never met formally," Aiden said.

How should she respond? *Me, too?* Since she'd determined to stay as far away from the Blackstones as possible, that would be a complete lie.

He went on, apparently not expecting a response. "There's no point in beating around the bush," he said, earning an eye roll from his wife. "Jacob told us what happened, or rather, why you left town."

He glanced at his wife, and they shared a look of momentary communion. "If Christina and I understand anything, it's how manipulative my grandfather was, how he set out to twist the world into his own version of perfect. But for the record, we look forward to you and Carter joining our family."

KC shot a glance at Jacob, wondering how he felt about all this. His stoic look gave nothing away. "I'm not sure how this will work out yet..."

Aiden shook his head. "Doesn't matter. If you need us, we're here."

Then he turned to talk to Jacob as if he hadn't just dropped a bomb in the middle of the park.

"How's everything comin'?" Jacob asked, seeming unfazed by his brother's words.

"Hartwell's doing a great job..."

KC watched as Aiden's hand cupped Christina's shoulder. He stroked up and down hypnotically, giving his wife his attention even while he talked to Jacob. The ache that bloomed deep in her gut didn't mean KC was jealous of the other couple. Not really.

Knowing that bridging this gap was up to her, KC wasn't willing to simply stand there while the men talked.

"Hey, Christina," she said, feeling awkwardly formal. If she was going to be around Jacob's family and regain her friendships, she would have to jump this hurdle. "How are you?"

"Good," her friend said. "Things are really good."

Drawing in a deep breath, Christina lifted dark, somber eyes. "Do you have any pictures of him? I haven't gotten to see Carter up close since you've been back."

KC tried not to wince. The implication hung in the air. It meant a lot to Christina that KC had cut her out of her life for the past year. Pulling her phone out of her back pocket, KC scrolled until she found the folder of Carter's pictures.

Then she held the phone out for Christina, hoping her willingness to share would start to repair the breach in their relationship.

"Oh, how sweet," the other woman breathed.

KC felt the motherly glow of pride she still wasn't quite used to spread over her. Then Jacob reached out and took the phone from Christina's hand. Turning the screen toward him, he started to scroll through the pictures. KC couldn't stand to look at him, the sadness in his eyes was so profound.

The guilt that had been growing over her decision to keep Carter from Jacob burrowed so deep inside she doubted she'd ever be rid of it. Yes, she'd been afraid. She'd been angry. She'd been pressured. But in the end, her choice to cave under James Blackstone's demands had deeply hurt Jacob. Now she got to live with the proof of that.

Finally he came to a single picture and stopped, simply staring at it. He didn't say anything, and the ache was made worse by his silence.

In an effort to escape, KC shifted her eyes, but found herself caught by Aiden Blackstone's hard stare. She'd heard he was a tough nut to crack, but the echo of his brother's pain she saw in Aiden's eyes told her she'd hurt not just Jacob but his family, too. A hard knot of self-disgust formed in her stomach.

"Let me show you what the construction crew is up to," Christina said, taking her arm to guide KC away.

Probably for the best. She might ruin her boundaries with Jacob by bursting into tears right there.

Not that being with Christina was much easier. She knew the minute her friend threw the first glance her way, then threw several more as they walked slowly away from the men toward the half-standing fort. The sound of electric nail drivers peppered the air. To the right, three men were securing a set of monkey bars into the ground.

"I really don't understand, KC," Christina finally said. "And I want to understand. I do."

"James threatened my family. I didn't know how to get out of that without hurting them."

"That part I get," Christina said "Trust me, I really do. My own experiences with James are numerous and traumatic."

KC could only imagine, living in Blackstone Manor with James while caring for his daughter, Lily, meant Christina had no way to avoid him. Lily required full-time care after a car accident had eventually led to a long-term coma. Christina's dedication to her patient and friend had put her at James's mercy. Then he'd forced Aiden and Christina to marry. Last year had been just as traumatic for her as for KC.

"What I don't understand," Christina said, "is why you

wouldn't come to me as your friend, ask for help, let me offer some kind of emotional support for you and Carter. Didn't you think I'd want to do that for you?"

KC stopped, afraid if she tried to walk and talk at the same time she might fall flat on her face. She wasn't prepared for this conversation, and sparring with Jacob took a lot out of her. "I am sorry, Christina. But I couldn't risk you putting two and two together."

"Putting two and two together? Honey, I had no idea you'd even met Jacob. How you managed to actually get pregnant by him is a mystery of biblical proportions."

KC had always appreciated that Christina got her point across in a ladylike but effective manner.

"Keeping our—" she swallowed hard "—affair a secret wasn't my choice. Only…afterward."

"Well, y'all did a damn fine job of it. I mean, I saw Jacob some when he was home all those times. I never had an inkling."

KC finally gathered the courage to meet Christina's questioning gaze head-on. "Which is not what I wanted. I never chose for our relationship to be this hidden thing. That was how Jacob wanted it, though I didn't realize it until after that first week. Somehow I knew, deep down, that Jacob wouldn't continue seeing me if we went public." So she'd bit her tongue and grasped at whatever crumb he'd thrown her, even though every secret encounter hurt more than the last.

"Why wouldn't Jacob want people to know about you?" Christina asked, shaking her head with the same confusion KC felt over it all.

"I suspect because he had no intention of our time together meaning any more than it did. When he came to visit, we would hang out and have, um, fun, but that's as far as it went. No invitations to dinner at a restaurant in town, no family dinners, nothing. If he wanted to go out, he drove me to Sheffield. What other message was I supposed to get from that, Christina?"

Her friend glanced back at the men over KC's shoulder. "I don't know," she murmured.

"It wasn't the type of relationship you bring something as permanent as a baby into." As much as KC wished it had been. "Not that I planned to keep Carter a secret permanently. I just hadn't figured out how to tell Jacob yet."

"But close friends are supposed to be there for each other. What about me? Avery? We could have helped you, KC."

"Asking you to keep this secret wouldn't have been fair to you. And James Blackstone would not have taken kindly to word getting back to Jacob. He made that very clear."

"Well, you weren't the first," Christina said with a grimace. "Thank goodness his days of manipulating others are over. Why didn't you come to Jacob as soon as you knew James was dead?"

Because I still wanted more than I could have. "It was kind of hard to figure out how to bring the subject up. Not that keeping it from him was ideal, either. But the important thing now is that Jacob and I learn how to work together for Carter."

She hoped her friend could see the sincerity she felt as she met her gaze head on. "And that you forgive me. Being without you and Avery these past months has been very lonely."

Christina hugged her, not holding back even though KC knew she still had to have reservations. After all, she was a Blackstone now. Who knew how this would all play out?

"I've missed you, too," Christina said.

KC closed her eyes and returned the hug. Her family had been there for her every step of the way. The aunt she'd gone to stay with had been helpful and loving. Really, KC had had a great deal of support. But she'd missed her friends. It hadn't been the same without them.

It hadn't been what she wanted. Sometimes, when she was pregnant, she would dream that Jacob was with her. Rubbing her back. Picking out names. Dreaming of the future. But she'd been too afraid to reach out for what she'd wanted.

She glanced back over her shoulder to see Jacob and Aiden still in an intense discussion. Jake's brows were drawn together, his eyes hooded. So far away from where she wanted him. She'd never have him now, not even the way she'd had him before.

Still, she'd make up for her mistakes with Jacob. Somehow.

Four

On the ride back to the house, Jacob sat in silence, wondering what Christina had said to KC. Their hug before they parted suggested it had been something good, but Jacob had been too caught up in his own emotions to track their conversation. He left KC to her thoughts as he tried to sort through the tangle in his own brain.

When they reached KC's house, there was a vehicle he didn't recognize parked in the driveway. This time, a Ford F150. Jacob felt jealousy make another appearance. Though plenty of women drove trucks in the South, it was usually a man's mode of transportation. What man would go into KC's house when she wasn't home?

They were barely inside before KC's mom appeared in the doorway from the kitchen. She watched him with wide eyes that made him ashamed of his threats to take Carter away. This woman was obviously afraid of his role in her grandson's life. Considering his grandfather's demands, Jacob could see why.

"Carter's asleep," she said, her voice hushed as if they were still in the baby's room.

"Thanks, Mom," KC said with a smile. "Did he give you any trouble? He's been a little fussy the past few days."

"As if that baby could be any trouble at all," her mother scoffed.

"That last time he got sick he screamed for hours," a man said, appearing in the doorway behind KC's mother. "Babies are cute, but trust me, they're trouble."

His mother glared. "Spoken like a true bachelor."

"Babies can't help it that their only form of communication is crying," KC said with dry humor.

The man in jeans didn't appear offended. Jacob studied him. He'd forgotten KC had a brother. Zachary, he thought was his name. Though his complexion was darker, his hair long and midnight black, those unusual hazel eyes were the same as KC's. After introductions, the men took each other's measure silently. From her brief mentions of him, Jacob remembered her brother worked hard to assist his mother and grandmother, full shifts at the mill, nights at Lola's and even extra gigs doing crop dusting for the cotton farmers around here. Hardworking and conscientious.

Ms. Gatlin eyed KC and Jacob both, as if wondering what they'd gotten up to while they were gone, then swung her gaze solely in Jacob's direction. The thorough inspection made him uneasy, but Jacob wasn't offering any explanations. Whatever KC wanted her mom to know, she'd tell her. Jacob just wished she would be on her way so he could finally meet his son.

Something he wasn't doing under the prying eyes of a crowd.

"Mom, I'm going to have to miss lunch this afternoon," KC said. "But we'll be there next week."

Her mother's look turned into a glare, but Jacob stayed silent. This was between KC and her family.

"Why would you do this, KC?" the older woman finally asked, turning her glare on her daughter. "Why would you give him full access to Carter?"

"Mom—"

"He's the enemy. Can't you see that?"

Offended, Jacob squared his shoulders, his back tightening. He felt as if he needed to jump to his own defense, to KC's defense, but the anguish in the older woman's voice held him back. He met the turbulent gaze of KC's brother as he placed an arm around his mother's shoulders. Jacob guessed her intensity had to do with more than just Jacob and the Blackstones. But he wasn't going to justify his right to see his son to anyone.

"Mother, he is Carter's father."

"Yes, and you ran far away rather than turn to him for help. What kind of father could he possibly be?"

Jacob wouldn't know until he was given a chance—

"I made a mistake," KC said. "It was wrong of me to keep Jacob from his son. I need to find a way to make that right. You knew he'd come into our lives when I moved back. Somehow."

"I can't believe you're just going to let him waltz in here and take Carter from us," she said, tears forming in her eyes, which were so like her children's.

Jacob couldn't stand it. "Ms. Gatlin, I'm not going to—"

"Why not? Old James sure did."

Yes, and Jacob was getting very tired of the reminder. "I realize my grandfather was a selfish man, a bully who had to get his own way. In his mind, threatening her, driving her away, meant he could control who became a true Blackstone." His conscience twinged as he realized he'd inherited some of that need for control himself. Still, Jacob stood a little taller. "But I'm not James Blackstone. The last thing I want is for Carter to disappear."

It was clear from her face that he hadn't made her feel better about him. "Then I guess it's a good thing she didn't take the money to abort him, isn't it?"

Jacob choked, heat flushing up his neck to his face. "What?"

Her eyes widened as Ms. Gatlin realized she'd gone too

far. She looked to KC, her mouth opening but no sound coming out.

With a resigned look, KC murmured, “I was offered a check. I could have had the money if I’d been willing to get rid of Carter for good. But I couldn’t.”

“And he just let you walk away?” Apparently there were a few things Canton had left out.

KC shrugged as if it didn’t matter, but her face told a different story. “As long as I abided by the rules and didn’t contact you, he let me go and my family didn’t have to suffer. He said, well, he said I was a rare find.”

“Why?”

“He called me an honest woman who knew her limitations. Coming from someone who’d just threatened the livelihood of three single women, it wasn’t really a compliment, though in his twisted way he probably meant it as one.”

Jacob could see how James would feel that way. He would have wished for her to take the permanent option, but as evil as James was, he would admire someone who held on to her integrity, even while he was crushing her will under his demands.

“So you’re not your grandfather,” Ms. Gatlin said, not willing to completely let go. “But I saw how you treated KC before. And you’re still a hotshot businessman, right? Always looking at the bottom line, aren’t you? How do we know you won’t take Carter and try to destroy us because we stood in your way?”

“You don’t. You simply have to trust me.”

“Men aren’t usually trustworthy.”

Jacob could see the shadow of pain in all three pairs of eyes. It was obvious the distrust ran far deeper than their treatment at the hands of James Blackstone. He glanced over at KC, seeing shades of despair on her beautiful features. Having lived in the same town as the Gatlins all his life, he should know this story. Sadly, he didn’t. And the fact that he had never asked drove home his own failings in his time with KC.

"Ms. Gatlin," he said, the fear in the older woman's eyes making it impossible for him to keep silent. "I assure you, KC and I are going to work this out in the best possible way *for Carter*. That is the goal here."

KC's mom looked skeptical, almost militant, but Jacob wasn't fazed. He only had to prove himself to KC. The rest would work itself out later.

"Fine, KC," her mother conceded, though she still sounded skeptical. "What about tomorrow?"

"Same schedule as usual," KC said with a quick glance his way. "I'll see you around noon."

Schedules. Another thing they'd work out later.

With that assurance, KC's mother and brother were on their way. Jacob remained rooted where he was while KC walked them outside. A deep breath in, then out, cleared away his tension from the meeting with KC's family. The silence seeped into him until he thought he could almost hear the whispering breaths of his son as he slept. Fiction, he knew. A product of his strain to connect with the son he hadn't known existed. Yet he couldn't move. Couldn't make himself walk down that hallway.

He could do this. He might not have prepared to have children yet, but it was like any kink in the manufacturing schedule. A good manager evaluated the situation, decided on the best approach and followed through. Right now, that situation entailed seeing his son up close for the first time.

KC stood talking to her mom out by her car. Turning away, Jacob took one step, then two, until he was in the short hall that connected the rooms in KC's tiny house. Having been in the house before today, Jacob easily guessed which room was Carter's. Sure enough, a little plaque adorned with pictures of painted tools, baseball bats and soccer balls was hung on the door.

Easing it open, Jacob peered through the dim light to

the white crib at the far side. His heart pounded as he registered the white noise of a small fan, the green walls and the mobile of stuffed dinosaurs in bright colors over the crib.

Despite the adrenaline rushing through his veins, Jacob forced himself across the small space. His first peek over the crib railings revealed an incredibly small…person. Splayed on his back, Carter slept with arms sprawled and legs kicked out at crazy angles. Jacob smiled. KC slept the same way. They'd never done the traditional spooning thing for longer than it took for her to fall asleep. After that, she needed her space. He wondered if Carter was just as grumpy in the mornings.

Carter's cheeks were round and chubby, his lips the same full bow shape as KC's. Those dark golden curls covered his head, prompting Jacob to reach out and slip his finger inside one with careful precision. His son. His *son.*

Though he hadn't heard her come in, he felt KC as she approached his side. He couldn't turn to face her, afraid the unexpected emotions swirling through him in this moment would be plain to see on his face.

"You can pick him up if you want to hold him," KC whispered. "He's still in the stage where he sleeps through a lot."

Jacob hadn't even known there was such a stage. He knew absolutely nothing about babies. His brothers had never had kids. His colleagues who had children didn't talk about them much; their existence was marked by no more than the requisite picture on their desks. Seeing Carter lie there, so innocent, so alive, showed him just how wrong that was.

But how did he do the fatherhood thing differently? He'd have to dig deep to remember his own father, those early years before their time together was stolen by James Blackstone.

His hand tightened on the railing of the crib, but he couldn't bring himself to move. Carter looked too small;

surely he needed special handling. Jacob didn't even know where to start.

As if she could read his body language, even in the gloom, KC reached over and scooped Carter up. Nothing more than a twitch of his mouth showed that he was aware. Not giving Jacob a choice, KC lifted Carter's small body to rest against his chest.

"Let his head rest in the crook of your arm," she said.

Jacob felt himself follow her instructions, easing the baby into position. He supported Carter's head with his elbow and placed his arm along the back of the child's spine. His hand cupped a diapered rump. As the warm weight settled against him, Jacob's other arm came around to hug his son close.

As he stared down, conscious of Carter's weight and fragility, something deep inside him sighed. He might be daunted by the task in front of him, but in that moment, he knew he wouldn't stop until he'd done the best he possibly could for the child lying so trustingly in his arms. This was no longer just a wrestling match about who would have custody of Carter.

Raising his gaze to the woman who had brought about such a miracle, despite all the circumstances, Jacob couldn't hold back the words. "Thank you."

As her answering smile doubled the emotion he was holding inside, he knew a moment of panic. Because if this new feeling he had was any indication, he wasn't going anywhere for a long, long time.

All the emotions and discoveries of the past few days had jumbled up inside of Jacob, creating a desperate need for activity. He'd chosen a doozy. Jacob pulled into the driveway leading to Blackstone Manor just a few feet ahead of the furniture truck from Booties 'n' Bunting. Good. He hadn't wanted to miss the delivery.

By the time Aiden showed up, Jacob had supervised the

unloading of all the furniture into the third-floor nursery. Jacob was there, surrounded by the parts of the sleigh-style crib he'd chosen, when his brother found him.

"Why is that the only piece of furniture that didn't come assembled? You know they have people for that, right?" Aiden picked up a railing and twirled it, testing the weight.

Jacob immediately stole it back. "*I* wanted to do this part."

His brother considered the room and all its new contents for a moment before turning back to Jacob. "This baby stuff has really gotten to you," he said.

Jacob didn't bother to answer. The evidence lay all around him.

"What about the woman? She get to you, too?"

Jacob really didn't want to talk about that—or the lack of consensus over the care of their son, though he hoped to remedy that soon. But the few moments he'd spent with Carter—perfection.

Aiden crouched nearby, watching as Jacob finished sorting the parts and then started to assemble the crib. When he spoke again, it was in a more serious tone. "What's it really like, Jacob?"

Jacob looked up, ready to throw out his usual flippant reply, until he caught sight of Aiden's intensely curious gaze. A lot had changed about his brother since his forced marriage…or maybe Jacob was just getting to see more of the real Aiden. Either way, there'd been more moments like these in the past year than there'd been their entire lives.

"You mean with Carter?"

Aiden nodded.

"Scary," he admitted as he tightened a screw. "Exhilarating, fun, messy…" He torqued another.

"Sounds a lot like marriage," Aiden said with a grin, dropping to the carpet on the other side of the pile of crib parts.

Jacob thought of KC—how exciting it had been to be

with her, addictive but unsettling, because she kept him so off balance. Not neat and tidy the way he'd set his life up to be. He'd thought he was the only man who felt that way. "I wouldn't know," Jacob said.

"Did I really just hear a man admit that he didn't have all the answers?" Christina teased as she walked into the room. "Surely that's a sign of the end times or something."

She bent over to kiss Aiden, her wealth of deep brown hair sweeping forward. Then she straightened and looked around the room. Jacob followed her gaze, wondering if the medium green walls, light wood furniture and race-car theme would meet with a woman's approval. His answer came with her smile.

"This is really beautiful, Jacob," she said. "I'll admit I couldn't resist a peek when the painters were here. But this furniture—it all blends so well together."

Aiden put in his two cents'. "That's female speak for it matches."

He ducked away from Christina's swat, rolling across the soft new carpet with a laugh. Jacob couldn't help but smile. He'd never seen two people so happy—especially not in this house. Miracles did indeed happen.

He thought he might just want a miracle of his own.

"So when is KC moving in?" Christina asked.

And that stopped the fun right in its tracks. "So far, she's not."

Christina and Aiden glanced at each other, sending a jolt through Jacob as he recognized that same form of unspoken communication he and KC were developing. Then Christina waved her hand around the room. "I don't understand. What's all this for if she and the baby aren't going to live here? Is she refusing to give you a chance?"

When Jacob didn't answer quickly enough, Christina gasped. "Jacob, you aren't going to try to separate them, are you?"

He didn't like the thread of panic in her voice any more

than the panic rising in his own throat. Especially since he wasn't sure whether it originated in thoughts of losing KC…or keeping her.

"We haven't decided what we're doing in the future," he said, trying to smooth things over.

"Obviously *you* have," she insisted, "or preparing this nursery would be completely pointless."

"Christina, don't interfere," Aiden warned.

"How can I not?" she asked, trembling in her distress. "KC is my friend. I realize she made a tough choice, a wrong choice, but separating her from Carter wouldn't fix that."

"I'm not trying to punish KC. Or permanently take Carter from his mother." Jacob glanced around the room, not able to put his thoughts into coherent words. Commitment with KC wasn't even on the horizon, but already his love for his son had solidified. At least he could have this special place to start building his own family, even if he didn't get the girl. "I'm not really sure what I'm doing here. I just…need this. And so will Carter, regardless of whether or not KC and I are together."

Christina had a warning for him, though. "That may be all it is, Jacob. You may have no intention of doing any harm. You probably don't want my advice, but there's something your two testosterone-soaked brains need to realize," she said, glancing at Aiden. "If KC sees this room, and it doesn't come with some form of commitment to her, too, she'll think one thing and one thing only. That her trust in letting you into her life with Carter was sadly misplaced because you planned to take her baby from her all along."

Five

KC stood near the guard shack leading to the mill factory grounds, waiting for Jacob to make an appearance. It had been a week, and they still hadn't come to a conclusion about custody arrangements. This couldn't be put off any longer. While she dreaded the outcome, the wait was killing her. She couldn't sleep for worry, and the last thing she needed with a baby and full-time job was no sleep.

That could make things very emotional, very messy.

Finally Jacob walked through the gates toward his Tahoe. The frown on his face spoke of deep thought, until he spotted her leaning against a tree near his vehicle. Then his stride turned determined, purposeful. Within a minute or two, he had pulled KC out of sight of the guard shack and urged her into the Tahoe's front seat. Her door closed just as the bell rang for change of shift.

"Still ashamed of being seen with me?" she asked.

Jacob paused before putting the key in the ignition. "Do you want our former relationship to go public like this?"

Technically, he hadn't answered her question, but she didn't argue because he was right. She didn't want whatever was between them to become public in a rush of twisted gossip. But she couldn't wait any longer to ease the churning in her stomach. She wouldn't admit to herself that his use of the word *former* made it churn that much more.

She didn't speak as he started to drive. She just fidgeted in the seat of the Tahoe, watching as raindrops started to hit the window as he gained speed.

"What's wrong?" he asked.

She forced herself to quit moving and speak her fears aloud. "Are you going to sic that lawyer on me?"

"You mean Canton?" He shook his head, his jaw tightening over his thoughts—whatever those might be. "No, KC. If he's never near my son again, it will be too soon."

That was promising, at least. "Another lawyer, then?"

"Why? Are you anxious to get it all in writing?"

Fear dried her mouth, postponing her response. After a moment, Jacob pulled over and turned to face her. The distance between them felt like miles instead of a few inches.

"Look. We can do this two ways." That no-nonsense look on Jake's face scared her even more. "We can decide between us. Or we can involve a judge and a lawyer."

And who would lose in that fight? She had a feeling she couldn't afford the same caliber of lawyer as Jacob.

"Like your mom said, I'm a businessman. I'm used to covering my ass with a contract." Despite his words, he reached out to push her hair back with his long fingers. The touch disconcerted her, bringing back feelings she'd rather leave buried.

His tone softened. "But this isn't a company we're talking about. It's a person. You've already proved that you value Carter more than money."

Startled, she met his inscrutable eyes.

"You could have had a lot of money and no hassle, but you chose to give birth to my son instead. I don't agree with how you did it. I'm just grateful that you did."

Her breath caught in her throat, but she finally murmured, "Thank you."

For long moments the magic of communion whispered

between them. KC's heart ached for more, but anything more with Jake was just a dream. A dream she should have woken up from long ago.

Finally he turned back to look out the windshield; rain pounded heavily on the glass. "To keep this amicable, I think we can come up with a schedule between the two of us and each have our own time. Don't you think?"

His words chased the intimacy away like wind against fog. "Wait. What?" she asked, shaking her head. "You want unsupervised visits?"

"No." He drew the word out. "I want Carter to live with me."

"Um, no."

Jacob didn't show a hint of anger, his face remaining blank. "Why not?"

She hated that he was so calm while she felt white-hot and shaky. "I've told you why, Jacob. I don't know what kind of dad you'll be."

"How am I supposed to find out if you won't let me?"

"We'll find out first, then talk about you having Carter all alone." She almost choked on that last bit, but forced it out. "Until then, you can see him at my house. We both can. That way I'll know he's okay." *And exactly where I want him to be.* But she needed to speak logically, not basing her argument on emotions. "Besides, I have everything a baby needs at my house. You don't."

"Are you sure about that?"

Fear trickled over her as she pictured him standing over the beautifully carved crib at Booties 'n' Bunting. He sounded way too certain. What kind of plans had he been making while she'd been wallowing in fear?

"Well, Carter and I are a package deal right now. And I'm not moving." This fight wasn't one she was going to lose. So much of what she wanted had disappeared, but not Carter. Never Carter.

"Then I'll come to you."

That didn't sound as good as she'd hoped. "What do you mean?" Oh, heck. Was she really starting to fidget again?

"I mean, I'm not settling for a three-hour visit once a week. I want to be with my son 24/7. If I'm not at work or in the shower, we'll be stuck together like glue."

She could feel her eyes widen. Seeing Jacob every couple of days was one thing. But constantly? "I don't think this is the answer."

He crouched closer, invading her space. "You're lucky I don't drag you and Carter to work with me. We are a family. It's about time we started acting like one." His eyes were dead serious. "It's time to decide, KC. One way or the other. I'm either with him or calling a lawyer. Your choice."

KC washed down the tables during the midafternoon lull. The bar was open for lunch on Saturday and did a pretty brisk business. She had a few short hours to get caught up on all the cleaning before the wildness of the evening began.

If only all the activity would drown out the worries over Jacob's ultimatum. He'd given her twenty-four hours to decide. She knew what she wanted—Jake at her house, in her bed, becoming the true family she'd fantasized about. But that wasn't what he was offering. And moving to Blackstone Manor…

The doorbell chimed as someone came into the bar. KC looked up, surprised to see Christina walking toward her.

KC's classy friend had looked out of place the few times she'd been here. But she was friendly and always welcome. KC couldn't think of a single person who didn't love Christina. She epitomized the picture KC had of a true lady.

Their eyes met, and Christina sent a tentative smile across the distance between them. At least one thing seemed to be working out. If she could just figure out this situation with Jake…

"Hey, girl," KC said. "You want something to eat or just a drink to cool off?"

"A drink would be nice. Thank you."

Christina slid onto a bar stool with ease despite her pencil skirt. KC's mom stayed and chatted for a minute before going back to washing dishes. KC poured up a tall sweet tea, knowing her friend didn't usually drink alcohol.

"Jacob says you're in a deadlock," Christina said after a long swallow.

"Did he?"

That shouldn't surprise her, but it did. Jacob didn't seem the type to do the confiding thing.

Christina grinned, looking more than a little sheepish. "Actually, I overheard him telling Aiden, who was grilling him." Her grin quickly faded. "Why don't you want Carter at Blackstone Manor?"

"It's not about keeping him from there, or keeping him from you. It's about—"

She couldn't force the words past her lips. This was about her heart, and not being able to trust Jacob with it. Which made it even harder to trust him with their son. The men who'd been a part of her life hadn't cared a thing about her heart when they'd walked out the door. Would Jacob do the same to Carter once the novelty of being a father wore off?

She looked down to find Christina's hand covering her own.

"I know," her friend whispered. "Trust me. I know."

Christina probably did. From what she'd told KC, she and Aiden had been through their own rough times before deciding they loved each other and wanted to stay married. KC was a little jealous of her friend's happily-ever-after. Because she had to face reality instead.

"He's not taking my child."

KC wished she sounded strong and sure, but knew her voice was a little bit weepy, a little bit pained.

"And why should he?" her mother said, working her way back down the counter to the two of them. "I still say men aren't to be trusted."

Christina winced. "Ms. Gatlin, I don't think Jacob wants to take Carter away. He simply wants a chance to get to know his son." She spread her fingers wide, studying the ring on her left hand for long moments before looking back up. "Listen, I don't know Jacob well, but I've seen him in action. He's hands-on with his mother and has been for years. Most men can't or won't do that. Not even for family."

She locked gazes with KC, her sincerity reflected in her expression. "I really think you can trust him."

With Carter? Or with her heart? What was she thinking? Jacob had already taught her not to trust him with her heart. But Christina was right. All those visits home hadn't been for KC. They'd been to visit Jacob's mom, sometimes for doctor's appointments, because she was sick or just to check in on her. Jacob cared about his family. And he knew how to take care of them. Shouldn't she give Carter the chance to know his dad that her brother never got? That she'd barely had?

"I can't risk coming to Blackstone Manor."

"Why?" Christina asked.

KC threw a sidelong glance at her mother, then turned her gaze down to the bar top. "It would just be uncomfortable. I mean, he would never take me there before. Going there now? It would feel like—"

Her mother leaned in. "Turning into his mistress?"

"Mom!"

Her mother picked up Christina's empty glass. "Well, that's what it would look like to everyone else."

She had a point. "Well, he can come to my house."

But her mother wasn't done. "So you're just going to take him back in your house, in your bed? Hasn't our life taught you better than that? Don't you remember how easy it is for them to walk away?"

"No, Mom. I haven't forgotten. And don't worry about the bed thing." She forced the words out, even though she almost choked. "I don't think I'll be ready for that in a million years." *Please don't let me make a liar out of myself.* "But it could be fun to watch him squirm on the couch."

Six

Jacob finished up a conversation with one of the line supervisors, then strode across a portion of the production floor that was down for maintenance. This company grew on him every day. Not because he had a passion for textiles, but because of the hardworking people. Some he'd known for years; some were part of a whole new generation coming to work at Blackstone Mills. For the most part, they were a dedicated bunch of locals who took pride in their product. Getting to know them better had been a privilege and a pleasure.

Now the question haunted him: Who would want to ruin all this?

Not far from him, a tall figure stepped out from a side aisle. Jacob had been so lost in thought, it took him a moment to recognize KC's brother, Zachary. Jacob halted abruptly, bringing him within inches of the other man. They were about the same height, and Jacob met his challenging stare head-on. Great. Another family supporter. *Not.*

Jacob didn't move, standing his ground with a level look. Since he'd moved into KC's little house two days ago, her family hadn't come around. Was this his official "talkin' to"? Zachary studied him with those hazel eyes, so much like KC's. Just as Jacob thought the tension might crackle in the air, the other man stepped back with a small nod. "Jacob," he acknowledged.

"Zachary." Jacob extended his hand for a firm shake. Neither he nor Zachary tried to assert too tight a grip. Just a simple acknowledgment of each other as equals. This might work out better than Jacob had hoped.

"You don't have to eye me like that, boss. I'm not here for the whole 'keep your hands off my sister' talk."

Jacob felt his eyebrows rise, and wished he could tell the other man keeping his hands to himself wasn't an option. At least, that was what he hoped. KC had called two hours before the deadline with her choice: he would stay at her house. Somehow it came across as her doing him a favor, as if control had been snatched away from him with those simple words.

As if getting settled in her house had deflated some of the uneasiness between them, he and KC had moved back into their more natural state of flirting with each other, skirting around the sexual tension that built every second they were together. It reminded Jacob of their first date, played over and over in slow motion. The surprising part was, he enjoyed the anticipation.

But KC hadn't made clear where they stood—hope still simmered despite the fact that he'd slept on her couch last night.

Zachary wasn't done. "Besides, it's a little late for that talk. Considering Carter and all."

"Yes, I'd say so," Jacob said, keeping his grin inside. "But I meant what I said at KC's house the other day. I want to do what's best for Carter. That doesn't include backing down or letting your sister off the hook."

To Jacob's surprise, Zachary smirked. "Oh, I think you're up to the challenge. Just keep your eyes open with that one."

"She can be a handful."

Zachary nodded, an understanding look in his hazel eyes. "The two of you did a good job keeping this a secret. Even I didn't realize what was happening for a long time."

"I guess Carter was a pretty big giveaway."

"For the family, yeah. I knew a couple of months before that," Zachary said.

That surprised Jacob. "Guess it was a shock."

"Yes, but I respect my sister too much to butt into her life."

That was a concept Jacob didn't run into very often these days. Most people were more than happy to meddle. He cocked his head at Zachary in question.

"KC is a self-sufficient, capable woman," the other man said. "With our family history, she's had to be. Why she would want to be relegated to the shadows, I don't know. But I assumed she had her reasons."

She hadn't wanted it—Jacob knew that now. She'd viewed the clandestine part of their relationship in a whole different way than he had. He'd anticipated each moment with her and could only focus on her when they were alone. He knew now it was a possessive attitude. Not only did he not want the complications of other people, he'd wanted KC to himself.

Just the thought had his heart pumping.

"That being said—" Zachary continued.

Here it comes. The brotherly rebuke was clear in Zachary's voice.

"I'll stand behind KC…however she needs me to."

Jacob nodded to the other man with respect. It took guts to go against his employer in support of his family. Openly and without apology. Without the stereotypical "I'll hunt you down with my shotgun" diatribe. Because Zachary was more worried about his sister and her needs than asserting his manhood.

"Good," Jacob said. "Family should stand together."

Lord knew his family had its crazy moments, but he and

his brothers were there for each other every step of the way. So why had he not included them in his relationship with KC until he was forced? Not even his twin brother, Luke.

The answer to that lay in a part of his psyche Jacob wasn't sure he wanted to explore further.

"Do you enjoy working here, Zachary?"

The other man crossed his arms over his chest. "Why? Am I about to lose my job?"

"Far from it." Jacob gathered his thoughts for a moment, glancing around the area to ensure they were still alone. He was taking a risk here, but his gut told him it was the right one. Lowering his voice, he asked, "What do you think about all the problems around the plant?"

Once again Zachary studied him, thinking before he spoke. Jacob's respect for him grew.

"Why would you trust what I have to say?" Zachary asked.

Jacob answered with a challenge of his own. "Should I not?"

Zachary nodded slowly, as if coming to a decision. "We've got some sneaky mischief going on. It's pretty hard to go incognito with this many people around."

"Are you speaking from experience?"

"Ex-military. Air force."

Hmm… That could come in handy. "Any ideas how it's happening?"

"It wasn't really my place to look into it."

"What if it was?"

Before his possible new ally could answer, footsteps sounded from down a nearby aisle. Unlike the normal rubber-soled work boot, this was the *clip-clip* of dress shoes. That meant management. Zachary fell back a step while Jacob stretched his shoulders, loosening the tension that was gathering there.

A familiar face appeared a little farther down. Mark Zabinski had gone to high school with Jacob. They'd attended the only private high school in Black Hills, where they'd both been prominent in Future Leaders of America and student government. A business management degree had gotten Mark hired as one of the daytime line supervisors. He'd moved up through the ranks to manage the accounting department, but hadn't been able to get any further than that. Jacob couldn't help thinking his enthusiasm for the return of the Blackstone brothers was a little too forced.

"Hey, guys," Mark said, eyeing Jacob and Zachary in turn. "Everything okay?"

Zachary didn't rush back to his station like an employee who'd been caught loafing. Instead, he held his stance, looking down on Mark from his superior height without a word.

Jacob watched with interest but also refused to rush away. "Yes, Mark," he said. "Everything's fine. Zachary was just explaining to me how some of the equipment worked."

Mark nodded with enough enthusiasm to shake his longish, eighties-style blond hair and started describing how the surrounding machines worked, causing Zachary to quirk the corner of his mouth in a look of almost condescending amusement. Mark didn't seem to notice, but Jacob did. He agreed with Zachary more than he could admit in front of an audience.

As soon as the other man took a moment to breathe, Zachary jumped in. "I'd better get a move on. Day shift is almost over and I need to shut down."

Mark nodded, his look of supreme approval hinting that the idea had been all his.

Zachary shook hands with each man in turn, but his gaze caught Jacob's. "If I can help with anything else, just let me know."

Oh, Jacob would be calling. A man on the floor was just what he needed, and Zachary's position and history made him perfect. He'd check with Bateman, just to be sure there wasn't anything else he needed to know about KC's brother.

Mark watched the taller man's retreat, then turned back to Jacob with an ingratiating smile that scraped along Jacob's nerves. The man insisted on kissing up when Jacob would be happier if they just treated each other as equals. "You sure everything is okay?" Mark asked.

"Sure." Jacob wasn't about to reveal what the last part of his conversation with Zachary had been about—or the first part, for that matter. Though he hated how much it reminded him of his earlier attempts to keep KC under wraps, he and Aiden had decided it was safer to keep the relationship quiet for now. "What're you doing down here, Mark?"

"Oh, just checking in. You know, sometimes you have to stay on top of people, make sure their work is up to par."

Jacob couldn't decide whether to question that statement or mention that Mark didn't belong in this part of the plant anymore. "Well, we're good down here. Let's get shift change taken care of, shall we?"

Because Jacob had a woman to get home to…

Seven

Jacob wished he could ignore his eager lead foot on the drive out to Lola's. As scenery flew by, he reflected on how KC was at work and Carter was at her mother's. There wasn't any need for him to be there. The fact that he'd promised her 24/7 wasn't a really good reason for him to be speeding down the road toward the bar.

His body knew only one thing: get to KC. He wasn't even sure why. His body wasn't going to get what it wanted, regardless of how fast he drove.

Still, he obeyed.

Luckily he didn't get pulled over by a cop before he reached his destination. Lola's was sparsely populated on a Wednesday, but patrons were trickling in after getting off work. Jacob joined them, waving a few hellos, and decided he'd find a table somewhere KC could see him. It couldn't hurt for her to know he meant business about their mock-family togetherness.

He wasn't being stalkerish. *Not at all.*

Shaking his head at how messed up his mind was, Jacob crossed the room. He let his gaze sweep the bartending area, not wanting to appear obvious. Until he noticed KC wasn't there. Instead, her mother straightened bottles behind the bar. That stopped him in his tracks. Unsure now, he waited a few minutes. He knew KC would walk out of the back room any time now.

Seconds ticked by… Nothing.

Letting go of caution, Jacob strode over until he stood front and center. “Ms. Gatlin?” he said.

She raised wary eyes to meet his, though she didn’t straighten from her task of refilling the bottles under the counter. A stubborn squint had replaced her earlier look of fear. “Yes, *Mr.* Blackstone?”

Cheeky. “It’s Jacob. Where is KC this evening? I thought she was working.”

“She was. Now she’s not.”

He raised his eyebrows at that cryptic answer. Definite carryover of animosity from the previous day. “May I ask where she is?” he said, pulling out his phone for a quick glance to make sure he hadn’t missed a call from her.

“Not here,” she said, her tone even tighter than before.

Jacob stood, frozen in a quandary. He had a feeling that, as was the case with KC, throwing his weight around would get him nowhere. At least with KC, the arguing was part of the fun. That didn’t apply here. Could he appeal to reason? Probably not. Ms. Gatlin was a mother, with a mother’s emotions. What should he do?

“Ma’am—” he started, not even sure where he was going with the sentence. Then Zachary stepped around the corner of the bar.

KC’s brother held up his phone, displaying the text message screen. He was a little too far away for Jacob to read the words, but he got the point. “She’s at home,” Zachary said, ignoring his mother’s glare. “Looks as though Carter started running a fever around noon. She’s taking care of him tonight instead of working.”

Torn between his irritation at KC’s mother for keeping that information from him and anger at KC for not letting him know, Jacob locked his emotions down tight. "Thanks, Zachary," he said.

He turned back to the door, his mind now on getting to KC's house, when Ms. Gatlin finally spoke. "Why don't you take some food."

He half twisted back, eyeing her over his shoulder. Part of him couldn't help wondering if she'd poison his portion—if she even gave him a portion.

She refused to meet his gaze but continued speaking. "Sick babies don't leave a lot of time for cooking."

She headed off to the kitchen, and the men shared a knowing look. Ms. Gatlin wasn't about to offer Jacob anything, but she wasn't a heartless woman.

Twenty minutes later, Jacob was finally on the road with his lead foot and a fried-chicken dinner for two. When he arrived, he could hear Carter crying from the porch, which gave him pause.

Then he shrugged. He could play the big bad man too macho to handle crying babies, or he could play the man big enough to step in where he was needed. Even if he didn't know what he was doing. Pride be damned.

Walking through that door was a tough step, but he did it. When he crossed into the living room, what he saw gave him pause.

He couldn't believe that a woman holding a sick, crying baby could be so darn cute. In pink sweatpants and a tank top, her hair haphazardly pulled up in one of those clip things, she looked frazzled and concerned. She bounced Carter gently in one arm and patted him on the back. He would have smiled and kissed her if she didn't look on the verge of tears as Carter paused in his crying to cough.

Spotting him in the doorway, she glared as if he was the cause of all the ruckus. So fussing at her for not calling him wasn't an option right now, either. They'd come back to it later. The noise pulled his gaze down to Carter, whose chubby cheeks were now flushed. The rims of his eyes were red, too, but Jacob didn't see any tears.

KC raised her voice as her eyes narrowed on him. "If you want to throw your weight around, I'm not in the mood, Jacob."

He could feel the frown forming between his brows and struggled to maintain his mask of calm. How could one child produce such a racket? "Actually, I'm here because I thought that's what we committed to. When I say 24/7, that's what I mean."

She opened her mouth, but he plowed forward before she could argue.

"What do you need?" It might be better to head this discussion off at the pass.

He saw a sheen of tears forming in her muddled hazel eyes. "Um." She swallowed hard, turning away for a moment.

Jacob gave her the chance to regain her composure. He took the food into the kitchen and lay the containers out on the table. Then he returned, grateful the cries had subsided to whimpers interspersed with snuffles. Who knew a baby's distress could shake a man's firmest foundations?

"What do you need, sweetheart?" Jacob repeated, keeping his voice as gentle as possible. "Do you need me to hold him?"

"No. He wants me," she said, patting and bouncing the baby in a set rhythm. "But he needs to eat. Could you make a bottle?"

As Jacob made up the formula, he knew he'd have to take this situation in hand. From what Zachary had said, KC had been with the baby since a little after noon. It was now a quarter past six. Her disheveled appearance and quick tears, unusual for her, spoke to her exhaustion, yet she still tried to maintain her superwoman front. He wasn't going to let her run herself into the ground and catch Carter's fever. She'd pushed him to the periphery of

Carter's care since he'd moved in, but today he'd be jumping in feetfirst.

Returning with the bottle, he helped KC settle into the overstuffed chair she and Carter usually cuddled in. A relieved look swept over her face as the baby took the offering without protest. "Good. I think the medicine the doctor gave me is helping. This is the first time I've been able to get him to eat with any appetite. His other bottle sat out too long, and I didn't have enough hands to fix more."

He let her talk out her frustrations. There wasn't anything for him to add. The tension relaxed around her eyes, and she took on the peaceful expression that entranced him as she watched Carter eat.

How on earth could he feel this attraction and need when her focus wasn't even on him? Where was the crying when he needed a distraction? "He's not the only one who needs to eat."

"Well, you'll have to cook for yourself," she said with a frown. "I've got my hands full."

Boy, cranky babies sure created cranky moms. Though it was probably like any bad day on a job with grumpy customers, only worse because the care was hands-on with no quittin' time. "I meant you," he said, leaning closer to catch her gaze. "I brought home food from Lola's. Your mom wanted to make sure you ate." He'd keep her mother's attitude to himself.

Her eyes widened for a moment, then she gave a tired grin. "You know what? I didn't even notice you bring that in." She ran her fingers over Carter's hair. "Sorry."

"No problem." Surprisingly, it wasn't. Her attitude didn't make him mad or eager to walk back out the door. An urge to face the challenge she presented rose within him. He would do this. Whether she wanted him to or not.

They sat in silence for long moments. Almost as soon as the bottle was empty, Carter drifted off to sleep. KC, too. Her long lashes rested against the purple circles under her eyes. She looked so fragile, awakening Jacob's protective urge once more. One he wasn't comfortable with but refused to ignore.

He carefully lifted Carter from her arms, stilling her with a firm look when she jerked up. "Let's get you something to eat," he said as he settled the baby in the bassinet that she'd moved into the living room.

"Yes," she agreed, though her eyes stayed glued to the sleeping child. "I should eat while he's out."

Jacob led her to the kitchen table with a firm hand. "He'll be fine. We're right here."

She dug into the food with muted gusto. Had she eaten at all today? Or had her entire focus been on Carter? As soon as she stood to clean up, Jacob was on his feet, too. "Time for your own bed, sweetheart."

"I can't go to bed," she protested. "Carter might need me."

"That's what I'm here for. You've had him all day. You rest." He led her into the dim back bedroom, where he could see the bed that had been the stage for so many hot nights with her. But tonight, it was for her alone. "I'll come get you if we need you."

"But what if he starts crying?"

"What about it?" His confidence was built on shaky ground, but she'd never know.

"You won't know what to do."

She was right, but that wasn't the point. "I'll manage. Now, into bed."

As if to show her defiance, she strutted into the bathroom and shut the door with a firm click. He wasn't about to leave, because sure enough she'd be back in the living room if he left the path unguarded. So he crossed the room to confiscate the baby monitor on the bedside table, then took up residence in the doorway so he could hear Carter if he woke.

When she returned, she had a vulnerable look on her

face and wore soft, comfy clothes, which inspired him to hold her close. Then he remembered the reason he was here had nothing to do with their previous closeness, and locked his knees just in time. But he wanted to—boy, did he want to—with an ache that dug into his gut.

"Promise me you'll come get me if he needs me," she said.

He met her worried gaze, shadowed with fear and exhaustion. "I promise if we need you, I won't hesitate. Now rest."

She crawled into the side of the bed he knew she preferred, and snuggled beneath the dusky-purple comforter that had kept their body heat cocooned so many nights before. He swallowed, his body and his mind wishing he could join her just one more time.

Then he turned away, closing the door behind him. Returning to the living room, he gazed down at his son, praying he could live up to his words.

"It's just you and me, kid," he said. "I told your mom I could handle this. Don't make a liar out of me, okay?"

KC shot straight up in bed, her heart racing as if she'd just run a marathon. What was wrong? Something was off. What—

Carter!

Barely noticing the dark outside the windows, she rushed down the hallway. Only as she skidded to a stop in the living room did she notice the most telling clue to her long sleep—silence. A single soft lamp kept the lighting dim. Jacob sprawled in her comfy chair, his legs splayed before him, his big body overflowing the space. But it was the baby sleeping on his bare chest that made the breath catch in her throat.

She stepped closer, noting the natural flush of Carter's chubby cheeks. The red of his earlier fever was gone. Jacob had changed him into a baby gown. As her hand rested on

Carter's upturned cheek, she didn't detect any fever. His sleeping face was turned up to his daddy's; his arm spread across Jacob's chest with his fingers curled into the light sprinkling of hair.

She couldn't resist the temptation. Certain that Jacob was asleep, she let her eyes wander over the muscled pecs that were usually hidden beneath his button-down dress shirts. He'd discarded his belt along with his shirt, but he still had on his navy dress pants, creating a dark contrast against his lightly tanned skin and Carter's creamy-yellow gown. Jacob's feet were now bare, prompting KC to smile. She'd learned that the one primitive habit Jacob had was stripping off his shoes and socks the minute he was behind closed doors. Unfortunately, his long, lean feet were as sexy as the rest of him.

A sudden wave of emotion hit her. Dreams from her pregnancy flashed through her mind. Dreams of a real family, of Jacob being with them, being devoted to them. Two days into his challenge, and already her fears of him abandoning Carter were dissolving like sugar in water. Which only opened up a new set of fears—after all, children were forever. Romantic partners were a whole lot more disposable. History had taught her that long before she knew what romance meant.

Yet one long look at the surprisingly sexy picture of her ex-lover and her son tempted her to forget her worries and take the plunge. Then she noticed Carter's lips pucker as if searching for a bottle. His little body squirmed. A feeding was about to be on the agenda. Her heart melted as Jacob's hand came up; he patted the baby's back without opening his eyes. Bittersweet as it was, the picture before her assured her Jacob wanted to be a part of Carter's life. He'd be a good dad, even if he wouldn't let himself be husband material.

Slowly Jacob's hand moved up to lightly brush Carter's forehead, a move KC recognized as her own in checking

Carter's temperature. She smiled, then looked up to meet Jacob's unexpectedly open eyes. For a moment she froze, held by the intensity of the emotions swirling there.

Anxious to hide her own feelings as her awareness of him soared, she mouthed, "When did he eat?"

With barely a jiggle, Jacob reached for his phone and checked the time. "A little over four hours ago," he whispered.

Suddenly eager to get away, she hurried back into the kitchen. An open laptop caught her attention. The geometric shapes of the screen saver floated back and forth. She shouldn't look, wasn't even sure why she wanted to, but she couldn't resist. A single swipe of her finger across the touch pad and the screen cleared.

Her heart contracted. Jacob had appeared confident and ready for the challenge of being left with Carter as he'd bullied her into bed. But the internet search on the screen suggested otherwise. *How to soothe a crying baby.* Bless his bachelor heart.

Well, whatever he'd found, it worked. She hadn't heard Carter all night. The clock now said 3:00 a.m. About time for Carter's middle-of-the-night feeding, if he was still on his usual schedule.

No wonder she'd felt dazed. She hadn't slept eight hours straight since Carter had been born. Of course, she'd have slept like a baby on that chest, too.

She'd just gotten the bottle heated when Carter woke in earnest. While she settled down in a kitchen chair to feed him, Jacob headed to the fridge. With his back turned, she didn't have to avert her eyes from the long line of his spine or the subtle ripple of muscle as he moved. The upper edge of a tattoo peeked from the waistband of his pants. Discovering that yin-yang symbol, which he'd attributed to his connection with his twin brother, had been quite a shock. A sexy shock. Conservative businessman Jacob hadn't struck her as the tattoo type.

Turning her thoughts from the ways she'd shown Jacob her appreciation of his body art, she tried to focus on the present. When it came to cooking, Jacob had only one specialty: omelets. She'd imagined him as having nothing more than eggs and cheese in his apartment refrigerator back in Philadelphia. She hadn't been far from right. Now he pulled out all the ingredients and arranged them on the counter.

"Why are you cooking at 3:00 a.m.?" she asked, even as the smell of bacon browning in the pan made her stomach growl.

And why couldn't the man put a shirt on? Hunger hit her hard, in more ways than one. Amazing how a full night's sleep could make her feel like a new woman.

"No point in me going back to sleep," Jacob said. "I have to be at the mill early for a management meeting. Might as well feed us before I get ready."

"Thank you."

He nodded absently, continuing to crack eggs into a bowl.

"Jake," she said, her husky voice catching his attention. "I mean it. Thank you for your help."

His gaze held hers, and awareness shivered across her skin. Then, in that wicked tone of voice she'd only heard when he was lost in the depths of arousal, he said, "My pleasure."

If she hadn't been awake before, she sure was now. Relief that Carter felt better distracted her from the temptation of the half-dressed man cooking in her kitchen. Having gotten a good sleep himself, Carter was ready to socialize. For once, his eyes weren't only for mama. The occasional noise drew his gaze across the room, searching for the man who had bonded with him during the long hours of the night.

That was what she'd wanted. Wasn't it?

The question haunted her as she ate. Finally, KC ran a hand across her son's sticky curls. At some point during the night, he'd sweat, then it had dried, leaving his hair thickened and clumpy. “Since we’re awake, I think it’s time for a bath, sweetie.”

Jacob watched as she readied the sink, setting up the baby bath and starting the water. “What’s that?” he asked.

“It just makes it easier to give them a bath when they’re this little and you can’t safely put them in the tub.”

She deftly got Carter stripped and settled. He immediately started to pat at the water and kick his little legs. Standing next to the sink, she let him play for a few minutes.

“Wow, someone’s feeling better,” Jacob said.

She smiled in his direction, trying to regain control over the seesaw of her emotions. Sharing moments like this with Jake was both a blessing and a curse. It was necessary to establish the relationship she wanted him to have with Carter, but a poor substitute for what she really wanted—for them to be a family.

“He loves me to give him a bath,” she said, adjusting the water so she could wet a washcloth.

With just a couple of steps Jacob closed in, his heat blanketing her side as he spoke softly in her ear. “If I remember correctly, so do I.”

His words sparked images in her brain: Jacob undressing her, leading her into the shower, bodies soapy and slick. She shook her head before the temptation could pull her under. Without missing a beat, she pointed the spray nozzle in Jacob’s direction, the water catching him by surprise.

“Down, boy,” she warned as satisfaction spread through her, along with laughter at his yelp.

A few feet away, Jacob froze, his eyes wide. Her little joke just made the temptation worse. She couldn’t pull her gaze away from the river of droplets chasing down Jake’s bare skin. As if he could read her mind, Jacob chased one rivulet down his chest with his thumb.

“Well, then,” he said, his gaze zeroing in on her smile. “If I’d known you wanted me all wet…”

Her heart skipped a beat. *Please don't go there.* She wasn't sure she'd be able to resist.

"I think I'll take a shower now, too," he finally finished.

She knew better than to open her mouth, because anything she said would be provocative, not productive. She focused on soaping Carter down, but Jacob didn't leave. Finally, she asked, "What time do you have to be at work?"

"I've got to call Bateman to find out exactly when he wants to get started. I left yesterday before he knew, and I wanted to see you—check on you and Carter. I told him I'd be in touch later."

Yes, but did you tell him why? Or were she and Carter still the best-kept secret in Black Hills?

Eight

Jacob had faced down corporate sharks who worried him less than KC's grandmother. Not because of size or strength, but the sheer tenacity with which she held on to her dislike of him.

She was like a Chihuahua, pint-size with sharp teeth, and determined to hold him accountable for missing some standard that he didn't quite understand. When KC insisted he call her Nana, because that was what everyone called her, he simply couldn't picture it.

And KC's mother—well, she had gone back from angry to afraid. The family gathered every Sunday for an early supper. Twenty-four/seven meant Jacob had tagged along. Every time he reached for Carter, Ms. Gatlin flinched as if he would whisk the baby away, with no thought to how it would affect anyone but him.

He refused to let their reactions stop him from holding his son, something he'd gotten much more comfortable with over the past week of nightly baths, diaper changes and bottle feedings. At first, KC had tried to edge him out, but he'd soon shown her that he wasn't one of those men who wanted to hand everything over to the *little woman.* If she'd let him, he'd have been with her every step of the way—pregnancy, labor and delivery. Despite the successful night he'd spent with Carter when he'd gotten sick, Jacob hadn't gotten her to the point where she'd let him care for Carter unsupervised, but they'd get there.

One way or another.

He'd insinuated himself into KC's and Carter's lives with a seamlessness that surprised even him. Still, they were living their lives as if they were skimming the surface of a deep lake, and Jacob was surprised to find himself dissatisfied. Something momentous called to him from the depths, but he still hesitated to dip his head beneath the calm to find the answers.

Although he'd sure appreciate not sleeping on the couch, which he had a feeling KC found secretly amusing.

As they settled down to a casual but hearty meal dished up straight from the stove, Jacob was grateful for Zachary. Another man helped bridge the estrogen river in the room. Too many women, not enough excuses. A little work talk helped create balance, though by unspoken agreement they kept themselves on general topics. Before they left, though, Jacob would need to talk to Zachary about a little industrial-reconnaissance mission. Fingers crossed he'd come on board.

Jacob had feared the timing of this meal, and sure enough, Carter started to whimper. Not a full-blown cry. His afternoon nap was the hardest to get him settled for—most other times he slid into sleep with ease. Something for which Jacob, inexperienced as he was, thanked his lucky stars.

When rocking the baby seat with her foot no longer worked, KC abandoned her plate to soothe Carter. The other women and Zachary continued to eat as if this was a regular occurrence. Jacob couldn't. Shoving in his last bite of Ms. Gatlin's incredible homemade peanut-butter cookies, he stood up and crossed to take the baby from KC's arms.

"Sit down and eat," he said. She'd barely had time to make a dent in her food.

"I'll eat in a little bit after I get him settled," she protested.

Jacob was having none of that. He repeated, "Eat," this time accompanied by a stern look. He lifted the baby from her arms before she could protest. Situating Carter snugly into the crook of his arm, stomach to stomach, Jacob supported Carter's legs with his other arm. He'd learned quickly that his son would wiggle those little legs enough to drive himself and Jacob crazy. So he tucked his son close, his hand covering most of Carter's back. A now-familiar rhythm of patting immediately took over.

Back and forth, Jacob took them on a stroll for a few minutes until Carter finally relaxed and slid into a light sleep. Then Jacob settled back into his chair at the solidly built table that showed a lifetime's worth of wear and tear. As the baby snuggled against him—one of the best feelings in the world, though Jacob would never admit it out loud—he looked up to meet KC's grateful gaze.

Spending a lot of time with a sleeping baby meant they'd started communicating with a type of telepathic speech. All Jacob had to do was make eye contact, and he'd be able to tell what she was thinking from the look on her face. No words had to be spoken. It was the most intimate thing Jacob had ever experienced with another human being. Even more intimate than sex. And right now, that hazel gaze told him he'd be moving from sleeping on the couch sooner than he'd thought.

"That's quite the touch you have there," Zachary said.

Glancing at the others, Jacob was disconcerted to see he'd become the evening's entertainment. Varying degrees of disbelief, suspicion and approval registered on the faces of KC's family members. Which left him feeling both disconcerted and, yes, a little smug.

Jacob smiled down at Carter. "Well, practice makes perfect."

A grumpy huff drew his gaze back up again. "The big question is," KC's grandmother said with disbelief in her voice, "does he have any staying power?"

Jacob had to admire a woman who wasn't afraid to speak her mind, wasn't intimidated by Jacob's money or status. Her only concern was her family, as it should be. Jacob's own concerns were now wrapped up in KC and Carter. Sometimes more than he felt comfortable with, especially in such a short amount of time, but he was adjusting. Mostly. He just had to stay in control.

"Nana!" Apparently KC wasn't as approving of her grandmother's candor. "Don't be rude to Jacob."

The older woman stared down the table at her granddaughter. "Are you telling me you haven't thought it? After all the women in this family have been through? Divorce and abandonment. Abuse and neglect. The only thing more important than a man who will stick with you is one who'll treat ya right."

Jacob could tell by her expression that she *had* thought about it. Had he given her any reasons to think otherwise?

Zachary broke in before KC could respond. "You make it sound like y'all are antimen," he joked, his expression clearly saying *what about me.*

Nana graced her grandson with a crooked smile. "You're the exception, boy. Not the norm."

"Nana," KC broke in again. "You can't judge all men by a few. There are good ones out there."

What about in here?

The hope in KC's eyes, which he could see even though she refused to look in his direction, made his chest ache. He looked down at Carter and thought about what kind of man he hoped his son would grow into. How would he want Carter to behave if he found himself in the same situation as Jacob? The idea blew his mind.

"That attitude will get you into trouble," Nana went on. "One man might just be an example, or even two. But four between us? The pattern is there." She waved her hand at each of the kids in turn. "Zachary's dad and his wandering ways. Your dad got tired of responsibility. My husband, David, and his drinking. So I thought a boyfriend would work better, and ended up having to take a fryin' pan to him after he dared raise his hand to me." She shook her head. "I think I'm justified in my opinions."

Maybe so. They did seem to have the worst luck. Or was it really poor choices? As Nana turned her knowing eyes his way, Jacob was again reminded of a toothful shark…or maybe a barracuda. Who could blame her after a lifetime of being left to take care of herself and her children, all alone?

"So what have you got to say for yourself, boy?" she demanded.

Jacob looked around at the faces of the Gatlin women—strong women who persevered despite being repeatedly abandoned—and admired them. They reminded him of Christina. His sister-in-law had an incredible talent for blooming where she was planted, despite all the odds against her.

"I don't."

The women met his refusal to defend himself with wide-eyed surprise. Zachary hung his head as if Jacob was doomed.

"Nothing I say will convince you I'm any different, Nana," he said, soft but sure. "Nor you, Ms. Gatlin. I'm sure all those men had plenty of flattering words that they used to get what they wanted from you, but I'm not a man of charm. My portion went to my twin brother, Luke. But I *am* a man of action—I'll let my deeds prove my worth for me."

The look of approval in KC's eyes, mixed with something fiery, told him he'd scored more than a few points with his words.

Still, the uneasy current in the room continued until after the table was cleared. Figuring the women needed some time to discuss him, Jacob followed Zachary out back. An unusually large garage occupied substantial real estate behind the house. As soon as he stepped inside, Jacob could understand why.

He let out a low whistle as he eyed the old-school Camaro on blocks in the middle of the room. "Nice. You do the work yourself?"

Zachary nodded. "It's relaxing."

"You'd get along really well with my brother Luke."

"I've never had the pleasure of being formally introduced to our resident celebrity, though I've seen him some in Lola's. I'd love to take a look at his racing car."

"He has a mechanic for his stock car, but he does a lot of work on it himself, too. Says it's soothing."

Zachary smirked. "I agree. But somehow I suspect you didn't come out here to talk to me about restoring cars."

Jacob gave a half grin. "Caught me." He paced a semicircle around the front of the car, letting the open hood and engine beneath distract him. "So how bad was it? What do I need to know about KC's childhood?"

"Why haven't you asked her?"

Jacob didn't need to turn around to see the condemnation on Zachary's face. He could hear it in his voice. "No, I haven't. Or I didn't, before. Now…" He shrugged. "I'm not sure we're ready for that kind of conversation."

"When you're sure, KC should be the one to tell you."

But conversations like that were easier to have while staring at cars instead of facing a woman's vulnerable eyes. Which was why he'd asked Zachary instead of KC.

Remembering the other reason he'd come out here, Jacob glanced over his shoulder. Zachary stood near the tool bench, twirling a wrench between his fingers. “Have you thought any more about our conversation at the mill?”

“Oh, yeah, I’ve thought about it a lot. Hard not to. I’m keeping my ears and eyes open. You’d be surprised how little attention people pay to Maintenance.”

“No, I wouldn’t. When I spoke to him, Bateman said you have a great track record. He doesn’t understand, with your outstanding military career, why you chose to come home.”

“And be just another man who couldn’t stick around to help my family? The military gave me a chance for an education I couldn’t have afforded otherwise. Now I have a decent job close to home and can be here to take care of my family on a daily basis. Something they’ve never really had.”

Which made Jacob all the more anxious to prove to KC that he could be there on a daily basis, too. And not just for Carter—heaven help him.

Time to get off this subject before his guts got any more twisted. “So you’ll help us?”

“I don’t really see it as helping you and your brother, or even Bateman. I’m worried about the safety of the people who work there, the security of this town. I think the more vigilant security team has helped shut down some of the problems, but I want to know how the saboteurs are getting onto the mill floor and tampering with the equipment.”

Jacob nodded knowingly. “So I’m giving you an excuse to do something you already wanted to do.”

Zachary grinned. “I’ll never tell, boss.”

Zachary may be helping them, but he was as cautious as his sister, and Jacob had a feeling the other man wouldn’t have hesitated to brush him off if he hadn’t already wanted to get involved. He was his own man, and didn’t apologize for his choices. Which made him a good brother for KC, and a good role model for Carter—

Jacob hoped Zachary didn’t end up being the only role model in Carter’s life. Could Jacob possibly live up to Zachary’s example?

* * *

What to do with a man you would alternately kiss or smack silly? KC could feel the conflict pulling her in two different directions.

"Thank you for letting us babysit," Christina said softly, as if she could read the unease vibrating along KC's nerves when she handed over her baby.

Christina snuggled a sleeping Carter closer, the move reassuring KC. She'd never left him with anyone other than family. And the fact that she'd only found out about this little trip an hour ago hadn't given her time to prepare her emotions.

Or pack her stuff.

"I hope I remembered everything," she said, sliding the overstuffed diaper bag off her shoulder and putting it next to the travel bassinet Jacob was setting up. "Carter usually stays with my mom while I'm working. It was easier to just outfit her house with everything he would need since he spends so much time over there." She couldn't hide a frown at the man who had sprung this idea on her without notice. "Jacob didn't give me much time to prepare…"

The scoundrel had the audacity to glance up at her with an unapologetic grin. What was he so happy about? He used to hate any kind of spontaneous decisions, unless they could be carried out in the privacy of her house. She'd be scared, if he didn't seem so pleased with himself. This was like a date…which she'd never truly had with him.

He'd even gone to the trouble of getting a sitter for it. Her married friends often complained about their husbands not doing that. She should be grateful, excited.

She kept telling herself not to let this mean anything, but her hopes rose without her permission. The past few days they'd shared many heated glances and deliberately accidental touches. But she'd been afraid to make the first move, to invite him back into her bed without an understanding of what he was really looking for here.

Instead, she waited. Where was all her spunk when she really needed it?

Aiden chimed in. "Oh, whatever we don't have I'm sure we can find up—"

Christina's sharp movement, seen out of the corner of her eye, pulled KC out of her distraction. "What?" KC asked.

Her friend simply tucked her arm securely back around the baby. "Aiden was saying we'll find it if we don't have it." She threw a wary glance in Jacob's direction. "After all, we'll need to learn what we're doing soon enough. We've recently started trying for a baby of our own."

Shock held her still for a moment, then KC rushed over. Smiling her excitement, she hugged her friend carefully around Carter. "That's wonderful, Christina. I'm so happy for you." Happy, and maybe a little jealous. Christina's world would be real, not the make-believe one she and Jacob had created.

"What about all the travel y'all will be doing between here and New York?" Jacob asked from behind her.

Aiden shrugged with a nonchalance that KC hadn't known any of the Blackstone brothers to possess. "Christina says we'll manage."

"I have no doubt she will," KC said with a smile for her friend.

Christina was one of the most capable women KC had ever met outside of her own family. She cared full-time for Lily Blackstone, the men's comatose mother, ran the household and was highly involved in the community. Now she was building a life with her new husband.

If KC had based her opinion solely on Jacob, she'd have thought inflexibility had been bred into the Blackstone brothers. Strict adherence to standards and procedures served him well in business, but not so much in relationships. On the other hand, Aiden was a successful art import/export dealer, now running his business in New

York from Blackstone Manor in South Carolina. Even with trips to New York, it wasn't an easy task. Had he learned to adapt on his own, or with Christina's help?

Of course, with a nickname like Renegade, Jacob's twin, Lucas, was a whole different animal. After all, it took a special kind of daredevil to take on stock-car racing as a career.

The conversation whirling around her finally came to a halt and Jacob ushered her toward the door. "He'll be ready to eat when he wakes up," he said, surprising her with the same last-minute instructions she'd been about to give. "Make sure Aiden gets diaper duty. It's the ultimate test of manhood."

Then they were out the door and walking to Jacob's SUV. "Are you going to tell me where we're going now?" she asked as he helped her into her seat.

"Nope." Stubborn man.

His grin reawakened the ache in her chest. He was so beautiful with the sun glinting off the dark gold of his hair. For a moment, time stood still as he leaned against the side of the car watching her settle into her seat. She could reach out and touch him, pull him close if she wanted to, but fear of risk kept her still.

Then the moment passed and he headed around to his side of the Tahoe. He belted in, then they started forward instead of back down the driveway as she'd expected. "Come on, where could we possibly be going back here?"

Without answering, Jacob drove around the impressive manor with its landscaped back lawn and down a rutted road carved out of the surrounding fields of tall grass. They meandered down along the fence line until they passed a cabin that looked as if it was under construction, then turned into some dense woods on the opposite side of Blackstone Manor from the mill. She'd never been on this side of Blackstone land. Their families obviously ran in different circles, so all her hiking and partying experiences with her friends were in the forest south of town.

"I wanted to give you a surprise," Jacob finally said, throwing her a teasing glance she felt all the way to her toes.

"I thought you hated those," she retorted. He did. She could tell by the small frown that formed between his brows whenever she threw him off balance. He'd often overcompensated when she'd do anything not according to his plan, reestablishing control over every situation. Not that she had a problem with him being in control; it was simply fun to throw a wrench in his works every once in a while.

He paused the SUV, glancing over at her with a look that threw her even more off balance. It was a look of lust and mischief with an intensity she hadn't seen in a long time. "Surprises might not be my favorite," he said, "but you love them. Don't you?"

Normally she did. Thrills like surprise birthday parties and unexpected gifts peppered her life because her family knew she loved them. Most of her friends knew it. She never thought Jake had wanted to acknowledge it.

Only this time the thrill was combined with nerves. Not because this didn't make her happy but because she didn't have the one answer she really wanted. Why was he doing this?

"You surprise me all the time," he said. "You work hard every day *and* night. I thought you deserved something special."

There was no escaping the sexy intent in his gaze. They'd been skirting around this issue for days. But if this was an attempt to take their relationship back to where it had been before Carter, was she willing to accept that?

Obviously nothing had changed since their affair, except the fact that they were living together and their families knew. He came into Lola's most nights while she was working, but they had only the most casual of interactions while they were in public. Barely any conversation. Nothing other people could construe as a *relationship*. But his eyes rarely left her unless one of his brothers was present.

While she hadn't gone out of her way to keep their involvement a secret, she also hadn't advertised it, either. That small, small girl still tucked deep inside wanted him to make the first move, signal to everyone that she was his and worthy to be presented as a couple.

The farther they drove, the more she could feel herself weakening. Jacob stopped the truck near a gorgeous little meadow beside the stream that flowed through Blackstone land. KC drew in an awed breath. The spot was gorgeous, lush with green clover, tiny purple flowers and even a weeping willow tree. A dreamy place perfect for outdoor seduction.

The question remained: Would she let him?

Nine

"You're not eating much," Jacob said as he watched KC pick at the potato salad on her plate. "Marie's a great cook. I thought you'd enjoy this."

KC had been behaving oddly ever since they'd left Blackstone Manor. He'd understood her nerves in taking the baby over there. After all, she'd never left Carter with anyone but family. But he was confident Christina would take good care of him, and thought KC would be more comfortable with someone she knew than with him hiring a sitter.

He simply hadn't been able to wait any longer for time alone with his former lover.

But KC didn't seem to be enjoying herself. She set down her drink and turned her turbulent hazel eyes his way. "I just—don't understand, Jacob. I mean, this feels like a date." She shook her head, her thick tumble of hair catching the sunlight. "Is it supposed to be? Because I honestly don't know how to respond."

Jacob aimed to keep it light. The last thing he wanted was to pressure her. "How else was I supposed to signal that I wanted to take what we have to the next level? I thought putting the moves on you over spit-up duty wouldn't be quite appropriate."

Her grin was just what he'd been aiming for. "What's the matter, Jake? Getting tired of the couch?"

He met her smile with one of his own. "Oh, a long time ago, believe me."

When she shook her head at him, he decided it was time to push just a little. "What? Wouldn't you be? Can you blame me for trying? After all, we are living together." *At the moment.* He shook the thought away.

"No, Jake, I don't blame you," she said, sobering. "It's just so like you to ask me. Most men would have let the heat of the moment take care of that for them."

"Considering everything that's gone before?" He shrugged. "That doesn't seem right. Besides, I couldn't get through life without a plan."

She nodded, a slight smile forming on her lush lips. "You're right. Having a plan is *so* you, Jake."

He couldn't stop himself from reaching out to trace the curve of her jaw with his fingertips. "You deserve the best, KC." And she did. After thinking about everything her family had been through, Jacob had been doubly ashamed of letting her believe she wasn't worth acknowledging. Especially since the whole purpose of keeping her a secret had been to keep his own life simple and uncomplicated.

Or had it? Going public would have meant exposing her to James Blackstone months before the confrontation that had sent her away. Would Jacob have lost those days with her if she hadn't been able to handle the pressure? And what about the community? Would they have been able to accept the differences between the two of them? Or would they have looked down on her as a woman who made herself conveniently available to him when he was in town? As accurate as that sounded, the truth had been a beautiful thing for him.

Suddenly he couldn't wait to get to his big reveal. "KC,

I need to take a trip." He gave her soft skin one more stroke before he pulled back. "I want you to come with me."

"The whole 24/7 thing?"

He shook his head, already picturing how that was about to change. "Nothing to do with that. I'm ready for more than just being your co-parent, KC. This trip—it would be just you and me."

She swallowed hard. "Where? When?"

"I need to go back to Philly for a fund-raiser, a ball for a charity I've been involved in helping for a long time. I'd love for you to accompany me."

Instead of the happy acceptance he'd been expecting, KC pulled back with a frown. "You want me to go to Philadelphia again?"

"Yes." He drew the word out, uncertain now. His memories of their one weekend in Philly were some of the best of his life. Weren't they for her?

"I don't think that's a good idea." She rose, pacing across the thick carpet of clover.

He watched her for long moments, not sure how to respond. Coming to his feet, he asked, "Why not?" Why did he have to choose a complicated woman to become involved with? Nothing was simple with KC.

"What's the point, Jacob?" She faced off with him, squaring her stance opposite his. "Nothing's really going to change, is it? I thought I could accept that, I really want to. But I think that might do more damage than I'm willing to accept."

What? "I'm confused," he said.

"I mean, a weekend in Philly for sex and a fund-raiser. I doubt you want to show me off to your high-class friends, but I'm guessing you'd feel guilty about taking another date. While here at home, I'm still only good enough to be kept like a hidden mistress." She hugged her arms around her waist. "I thought I could live with that, but—no thanks, Jacob."

As he took in KC's obvious distress, Jacob winced.

"I'm sorry, KC," he said, swallowing past the lump in his throat. He closed in, wrapping his arms loosely around her. He needed to touch her, for her to feel him, but he still wanted to look into those hazel eyes as he told her the truth. Hopefully, she'd believe him.

"I'm really sorry for not realizing how much this was like, well..." He swallowed again when she raised her eyebrows. "How this was exactly like before. But that wasn't my intention. I'm trying to keep you and Carter safe."

"What?" she asked, tilting her head as if she hadn't heard him right.

"I forgot you weren't here when Christina was hurt."

Surprise stiffened her body. "Hurt? What happened?"

"There was a fire. Aiden's studio at the back of the property. The one that's now being rebuilt. Some guys set it on fire, not realizing she was inside. They were trying to strike out at Aiden, but she got caught in the cross fire. She could have been seriously injured if Aiden hadn't gotten there in time to get her out."

"Oh, my goodness. I didn't even realize."

Jacob could read the regret on her face. Christina had told him that the two of them had been estranged since KC's return. Which was also his fault, since KC had been afraid of telling Christina the truth and putting her in an uncomfortable situation.

"Aiden and I talked right after I found out about the baby. He mentioned that, since things were still unsettled at the mill and I'm a prominent figure over there, I might want to keep my connection to you quiet for now. That way you and Carter won't become a target if someone is upset with the way I'm handling things."

"So you think we'd be in danger?"

"I don't want to think so, but I also don't want to take that chance."

She paced away, leaving him feeling empty and cold.

KC had never been predictable, so he should have known she'd come back with something he wasn't prepared for. It wasn't long before she said, "So you talked about this with Aiden?"

"Yes."

"And when were you going to talk about it with me?"

Working with the public, and drunk people in particular, KC had become pretty good at reading between the lines. And the surprise on Jacob's face gave him away.

He wasn't going to discuss it with me. It hadn't even occurred to him.

At least, not until he was sure he wanted this relationship to be about the two of them, not just about Carter. Although, he hadn't lied about it. That much was good. KC's dad had been a chronic liar, hurting them all time and again before he left.

"Jake, you can't expect to make decisions that involve me or Carter without my input. Regardless of what happens between us as a couple, we're going to be working together as Carter's parents for many years. If we're in this together, as a couple or not, you have to be open with me. Leaving me in the dark doesn't build trust."

He moved close, rubbing his hands up and down her arms. "I didn't think about it that way. I didn't really think of it at all, to be honest. I'm sorry."

"And how can I be diligent and protect my son if I'm not aware of the danger?"

His slow blink of surprise told her that had never occurred to Jacob, either.

"As much as we've labeled this 24/7, you can't be with us all the time, Jake. I need to know what's going on." She couldn't stop herself from taking a step back, then another until his arms dropped to his sides. "I'm not a doll to be moved around at will. I spent a lot of years dependent on other people's bad decisions. I will not have that for my son…or for me."

"You deserve better than that, KC," he said. "I know that now."

When he turned away, she didn't know what to expect. From the way he rubbed the back of his neck, she knew he was thinking hard. She'd watched him do that so many times, her heart ached. She knew, deep down, Jacob was a good man. But was he the type of man she could depend on?

When he turned back, his expression was more open than she'd seen anytime outside of a bed. "I want you, KC," he said, his voice gaining strength as he went on, "I want to take this to the next level. But I also want to protect both you and Carter until this situation at the mill is resolved. People knowing that I'm living at your house doesn't make you safe. So for now, I'd like to keep it just like we've been doing, with only family and close friends who know just how involved we really are."

A sinking feeling hollowed out her chest, but she kept still. Her response would determine where they went from here. Could she make the right decision—for Carter *and* for herself?

"But only for now," he added. "Do you agree?"

Was it what she wanted? *No.* Could she argue with his desire to keep her and their son safe? *No.*

"Yes, Jacob," she said, smiling as she thought over the past thirty minutes. Most men would have simply taken her to bed and left the rest up in the air. At least with Jacob, she knew there was a plan even if she wasn't sure what it was yet. "I'll go to Philadelphia with you."

His relief was almost palpable. He rubbed his hands together, obviously wanting to reach for her. Instead, he motioned to the food. "Shall we finish eating?"

That little streak of mischief resurfaced, and she couldn't help giving it free rein. "Actually, I thought we would celebrate." After all, they'd just made a pretty big decision. Why hadn't he reached for her yet? Didn't he realize she wanted him?

"What do you mean?"

Bless his heart. This man desperately needed to let loose every so often. Luckily, KC knew the perfect way to tempt him.

"Jacob, we're in a secluded spot and alone. No baby. No audience. What do you think I mean?"

Just one look from Jacob turned KC to jelly. But she wasn't giving him the upper hand yet. As he stalked closer, she whipped her T-shirt over her head. Jake slid his tongue across his lips in anticipation.

He stopped just out of her reach, watching the show, his body tense and ready.

She unbuttoned her shorts, pushing them over the curve of her hips while she slid out of her shoes. Jake's gaze followed her every move. Next, she whisked away the tank she was wearing under her shirt. She watched as Jacob made a long, slow perusal of all her new curves.

The need that filled his eyes whenever he took her was the most naked emotion she'd ever seen in him, and she'd ached to see it again. There it was. Before, these had been the only moments she'd felt she was seeing the real Jacob. Since her return, she'd only seen him show unguarded emotion when he held Carter.

She'd missed this, missed him. Turning away, she shucked off her bra, releasing her breasts, which were much rounder since she'd given birth. She threw the garment over her shoulder and made for the stream nearby. On her way, she tossed her best come-hither look his way, marveling at how his gaze was glued to her backside.

Her first step into the cool water felt good in the early-summer heat. The chill traveled up her skin as she waded into the stream. Her arousal rose along with it. The liquid surrounding her soaked into the silk of her panties, which she knew would color them transparent. Her nipples peaked, and she covered them with her arms, protecting them from the cold and from Jacob's gaze.

When the water was finally waist high, she turned back toward the shore. She took in the dirt beach with its tangle of tree roots, then Jacob's bare feet in the clover, then his gaze as he devoured her from his higher vantage point. "Aren't you going to join me, big boy?" Her mouth watered at the thought of those clothes coming off.

He shook his head. "You are crazy."

"Maybe," she teased. Then she let her arms ease down until nothing was left to the imagination. "But I'm fun. Don't you remember how to walk on the wild side?"

She hoped so, because she was desperate for him to walk with her once more.

To her intense delight, he grabbed the hem of his T-shirt, easing it up and over his shoulders. When clothed, Jacob seemed to have an average build. But underneath all the fabric were beautifully sculpted muscles that made her heart pound and her core ache. He was all leashed power… until he loosened the reins.

From her vantage point, she got to see every sleek line, every flex of muscle. The ripple of his biceps as his hands gripped his waistband. The bulge of his pecs as he opened his fly, then pushed his pants and briefs down to the ground. The chill of the water and the magical surroundings receded as memories of his body flooded her brain. Powerful hips. Muscled legs. And the hardness jutting from the cradle of his hips, the part he used to drive her over the edge into insanity.

He stood unashamedly in the dappled sunlight, and she wanted to weep for the brief time she'd likely have him. She had no doubt that one day he would leave her, but she'd savor him while she could.

For now, he was all hers.

Ten

Jacob barely noticed the temperature of the water as he stalked toward the naked angel before him. Heck, he was surprised steam didn't rise from the surface, considering the fire burning beneath his skin.

Before, he'd only known sexy KC. Whenever he'd seen her, the dark temptations beneath her surface called to him on every level. So much so that the pull had remained even after she'd left.

Living with her, seeing her with their son, highlighted a whole other side only hinted at before—the angelic woman who went out of her way to love those around her, do whatever she could for them and help with any needs she saw. That was KC, too.

One part angel, one part danger…wrapped up in the body of both. It was a combination he couldn't walk away from again, but he'd worry about that another time. For now, he was eager to learn that body all over again. Leave the emotions for later.

As he got close, she ducked to the side, evading him as her laughter tickled the air around them. With a grin, he gave chase. He'd never had so much fun as with KC—not even with his brothers. It seemed right now, that was exactly what she wanted.

They played tag for a few minutes, forging against the water in a strategic game of Keep Away. Jacob had never enjoyed another view as much as the water parting around KC's waist, her naked breasts swaying with her movements. All too soon, watching wasn't enough. His hands burned for a touch.

With a heavy lunge, he grabbed her. Dragging her body up against his, he clamped down on his urge to emit a primitive howl. Heat instantly sparked between them. Jacob caught the laughing look in KC's hazel eyes. Her long lashes sparkled with water droplets.

His body automatically reacted to hers, even while his hands cataloged all the changes since the last time he'd held her like this. Her waist, slightly thicker. Barely there stretch marks beneath his thumbs from carrying Carter. A rounder curve to her hips that matched the rounder curve of her breasts.

"Like what you see, Jake?" she asked, her look turning mischievous.

Ah, the temptress was here, all right.

"Oh, I like what I see," he said, letting his gaze slowly inventory all the sweet flesh down to where she was pressed against him. "But does it taste as good as I remember?"

She squealed as he lifted her in his arms, carrying her to the shore with quick strides. His body wouldn't wait much longer. Her arms tightened on his shoulders as he climbed the bank, then strode across the carpet of clover. Now his angel sparkled all over as the filtered sunlight highlighted the water droplets decorating her body.

He spread her out on the blanket, then sat back on his heels for a longer look. His breath hissed through clenched teeth. *Gorgeous*. She released her hair from the clasp, and it spilled around her head in waves of blond. Her firm, shapely legs tempted him closer. Her perky little toes with nails painted pink made him smile.

She was the incredible mother he'd come to know. The sexy temptress he ached for. All his. Right now.

She lifted her arms toward him, and his eyes met hers. He saw the vulnerable streak of emotion there, as if she, too, could sense that they trembled on the brink of something new. She opened her arms, hiding nothing.

Jacob crowded over her, his legs firmly straddling one of hers. His erection was pressed against her thigh, causing him to suck in his breath. So sensitive, as if too much pressure would end their encounter too soon—a worry he hadn't had since high school. Unwilling to lose the moment, Jacob started in on her plump, succulent lips.

He took his time with the kiss, tracing the outline of her mouth before their tongues tangled. Then his hips surged forward, and he couldn't hold back his groan.

Her hands found his shoulders, pulling him down. Sucking him under as their bodies met and melded. He heard the catch in her breath, followed by a soft whimper, and his brain swirled with all the times he'd heard that same sound before.

He ached to jump ahead but forced himself to slowly reacquaint himself with all his favorite places. Only this time, his heart beat faster, her scent made him dizzier and his need pounded higher than ever before. Because this was KC.

And everything about her captivated him.

His heart should have stalled at the revelation, but his need wouldn't allow it. Instead, he slipped on a condom and eased his body into hers, savoring every inch. She'd been partly right: this was one of his favorite positions. Because he could take in every nuance of her expression while his body drove them both wild.

He pulled back slowly, then drove in hard. Her cries filled the sun-heated air around them—a sound Jacob knew he'd never forget. Over and over, he teased them both while his tongue traveled from nipple to nipple. He savored her taste, her sound, her passion. And finally her ecstasy as her body clamped down on his.

Letting himself lose control, he pounded into her until only one thought remained. This was more than simple lust, but could he break past the fear and admit what it truly was?

In the week since their picnic, KC had more than enjoyed reacquainting herself with Jacob. She'd treasured every second they were together. He was everything she remembered and more, as if the long months without each other had only heightened his appetite. They had definitely heightened hers.

But intimacy with a baby in the house was a lot different than when she was a single woman, so KC was pretty sure Jacob had planned on enjoying a free-for-all during their weekend in Philadelphia. Starting as soon as they crossed the threshold.

He had another think coming.

They were barely through the door of the hotel suite and he was already marching her across the tiled floor with his signature heated look. She wanted to give in, truly she did. But they needed to start off on the right foot, so she put up a figurative roadblock. "Where should we shop for my dress?"

Jacob's look was incredulous. "We have baby-free time and you want to shop?"

Men. Everything had to revolve around sex. "I didn't have time before we left town, and you promised..." She deliberately drew out the word, paired with a look of wide-eyed innocence.

He studied her, giving her the impression he could divine every thought. "You. Are. Serious."

You bet your booty, buster. The ache in her core betrayed her, but she refused to give in. “I told you, this trip wouldn’t be like the last time.”

“I don’t see what the problem was, honestly.” He leaned back against the wall with his arms crossed over that wide chest. *And here we go again with the Dom stance.* “I thought we had a wonderful time.”

“We did have a wonderful time. At your apartment. Having sex. The only time we left the house was to get to and from the airport.”

She could see the revelation steal over him, but still he tried to bluff his way out of it. “And that was a problem because…?”

“Depends.” Standing her ground, she faced off with his seeming nonchalance. “Do you want me here just for sex? Or for something else?” She couldn’t make him prove his commitment at home, not so long as she and Carter could be hurt by taking the relationship public. But here in Philadelphia, she could take a stand.

She wasn’t backing down.

His disappointment was almost palpable, and she found an echo in her own body. Maybe she should tell him he’d definitely be getting lucky, just not this instant? She quickly tossed aside the idea. She wasn’t sure whether she was just being mischievous, or whether she really wanted him to pay. Either way, it wouldn’t hurt to let him suffer for a little while.

“The ball is tonight,” she reminded him as they took the elevator to the lobby. “I don’t have a dress. And you said we had plans for this afternoon, so…”

He hailed a cab, then held the door open for her. “Will it take all morning to find a dress?”

“There’re only two hours left in this morning, but we’ll have to see…”

His poor-puppy-dog expression was so very cute, but he’d live. Even if he didn’t think so.

The cab dropped them off at a side street filled with

adorable little boutiques. KC wandered for a bit, peeking into window after window, unwilling to admit to Jacob that the high-priced surroundings made her feel inadequate. The only time she'd ever shopped for a formal had been for her junior and senior proms—she had found both dresses at consignment stores. Somehow she thought this would be a whole different experience.

Pausing before a window display of beautiful dresses, each decked out with a unique flare, KC knew she'd found the right place. She turned to Jacob. "I'm going to go in here and look around. I'll be out in a while."

He frowned. "I can't go in with you?"

Poor thing. Nothing about today was going according to his plan. "Nope. I want my dress to be a surprise."

"But I'm planning on paying for it." His satisfied expression said he'd hit on the perfect workaround. "That's kind of hard to do from out here."

"No need. I'll handle the bill myself—"

"No." If she didn't know Jacob very well, his scowl would have had her stepping back. "This trip was my idea. I want you to buy whatever you find that you love and not worry about the cost."

Her spirit rose up in protest, but he held up a hand. "No arguments, KC. Pick out what you want, have the saleslady ring it up, then come and get me. I'll take care of the rest."

Blinking, KC didn't know how to respond. Not only was he going to pay for her to have a dress, but he wasn't pushing his way inside when he could have. She swallowed hard. "Thank you, Jake."

He shot her a grin. "You're welcome. Besides, I'm building up brownie points."

I bet. She moved to the door, only to look back over her shoulder when he said, "Shoes and a bag, too. No arguments. Don't make me ask for an itemized statement as proof."

"Yes, sir," she said with as much cheek as she dared, then headed inside.

Contrary to her concerns about being treated as an inferior, the two women in the store were more than helpful, taking it upon themselves to find her the perfect dress for the ball. Both had heard about the event, so they knew exactly what she needed. After a couple of tries, KC found something that had her grinning like a buffoon at herself in the mirror. "Oh, yes, this is it."

"I agree," one of the salesladies said from behind her.

The black dress was anything but ordinary. A flesh-colored silky layer was overlaid with a transparent black lace appliquéd with black roses, showcasing glimpses of the flesh tones underneath. The bodice had a deceptive plunging neckline that cupped her abundant curves and provided support at the same time, the décolletage formed by the uneven edges of rose petals and vines entwined throughout the intricate layer of lace. The neckline was echoed in the low scoop in the back, and the hem fell to the fullest part of her calf. Here again the material's uneven edge gave the dress a uniquely strong, sexy look that KC found flatteringly feminine. Jake would love it as much as she.

Twenty minutes later, she had shoes, stockings and a small clutch to match, along with a filmy shawl to protect against the cooler evening air. The saleswoman added everything up and stowed the dress in a garment bag before Jacob was led into the store. Without a single question, he handed over a credit card, his cooperation earning matching smiles from his audience.

"You're gonna love it," the saleslady assured him.

Reaching around KC's waist and pulling her snug against his side, Jacob placed a light kiss on her neck, just below her ear where he knew she was sensitive and the touch would bring on chills. While she was still recovering, he said, "I'd love anything on her."

"Yeah," she joked, unsettled by this public display of affection. "He even loves my T-shirts covered in baby spit."

"Men love anything that highlights your, well, cleavage," the redhead said with a wink.

KC's heart melted when Jacob blushed. Yeah, she knew exactly how he felt about her boobs.

The brunette grinned at them before adding, "Nah, accepting you no matter what you look like is a sign of true love."

As they walked away, KC wondered with a touch of panic how right she was.

Eleven

Jacob's breath stuttered to a stop as KC breached the doorway from the bedroom. She hadn't been kidding when she'd said her dress would be well worth the anticipation.

Boy, had he anticipated.

The saleswoman's comments had kick-started his libido, making him wish for X-ray vision to see through the garment bag. Then, from the dress shop, they'd gone to a nearby lingerie store for the proper undergarments, which consisted of a smooth satin corset and matching panties. Was she trying to kill him? Then they had a late lunch; all throughout, KC's sexy persona was turned up high.

Just when he thought he couldn't take any more, he found himself pacing the suite and ignoring his work while she had her nails done in the hotel salon. It hadn't been how he'd pictured their first day in Philly, but now…now his body and mind slipped into overdrive as he soaked in her beauty.

If anything could capture his dual vision of KC as both angel and sex goddess, this dress was it: black flowery lace and flesh-colored fabric gave the illusion of lingerie, yet she was technically covered from chest to midcalf. Of course, knowing what she had on underneath tipped the scales in a dangerous direction. But the steamy look in her eyes—now turned a deep green—warned him that was part of her plan.

Her inner and outer beauty stole his breath. The intensity of his need sparked a touch of fear, but he quickly brushed it away.

He was tempted to persuade her to stay in—skip the reason they were here and give him a chance to peel her out of that dress and the lingerie he knew was hidden underneath. But one look at the tentative excitement on her face shut down his desires without a word.

I'm good enough for sex but not allowed into any other part of your life. Back in Black Hills, he couldn't openly acknowledge his relationship with her and Carter without endangering them. But here, he could take her out in public with pride.

He was ashamed that she had believed he viewed her only as a sex object. He would never demean her like that again.

"You are incredible," he said simply. "I couldn't be more proud than to have you on my arm tonight."

The faint uncertainty in her expression fled, and she glowed under his praise. But soon enough that saucy look returned. "I do believe you'll be rewarded for your kind words, sir…later."

Her husky promise sent him back into overheated territory. He hustled her out of the suite and away from the bed before he proved himself a liar.

Never had the dichotomy in KC's personality been more evident to Jacob than in the crowded ballroom, where they were surrounded by men and women Jacob had been doing business with for years. The lights sparkled off tiny jewels embedded in each flower on her dress, and she shone like the star she was as she conversed with an ease that shouldn't have surprised him. After all, he'd seen her calm the most ruffled of feathers at Lola's. Here she was an angel, but Jacob could read the latent sensuality in the graceful movement of her body and the continual meeting of their eyes. Hers held a promise. Which turned to surprise when his name was called from the stage.

"We are happy to honor all the board members for their hard work for a charity that goes above and beyond in caring for children and their families as they receive the medical treatment they need. Jacob Blackstone, our chairman, would you please make the presentation tonight?"

Jacob cursed in his mind. He should have remembered this part and prepared KC. He'd been more focused on having her here than on the presentation he'd made numerous times.

After announcing how much money the event had raised for the charity, and giving the usual plea for continued generosity, Jacob returned to KC's side. Only there was no time to explain as one person after another came up to talk.

Finally Jacob swept her to the dance floor, taking advantage of a few moments of privacy. Of course, he was fooling himself if he didn't admit he was eager to hold her close once more, even if he couldn't take what his body was begging for. Still, his fingers savored the bare skin of her back in the dim lighting.

KC, with her usual no-nonsense attitude, went straight to the point. "That was a surprise. I guess I should have done a Google search of you before we dated, found out how important you were everywhere, not just in Black Hills..."

"I'm sorry, KC. I should have made it clearer that I was the chairman when I asked you to come with me. I just wasn't thinking—"

"About more than getting into my pants?"

He choked back a laugh but couldn't help the big grin that split across his face. "Guilty."

It was a much more rewarding subject of conversation, in his opinion. "Have I told you how beautiful you are tonight?" *And every night?*

He savored her upturned face, that gorgeous hair swept to the top of her head, giving him a view of the vulnerable parts of her neck where he knew a simple kiss would have shivers running along her body. They moved in time to a classic slow dance, their bodies barely brushing against each other.

Good thing. Jacob didn't want to embarrass himself.

"This is incredible," KC said, her wide-eyed gaze taking in the crystal chandeliers suspended from the ceiling and the glittering decor that sparkled in the strategically dim light. "Way better than the Under the Sea theme from my senior prom."

They shared a grin.

"Yeah, the committee goes out of its way to create a very special night. We have a wonderful coordinator, and she makes it well worth the amount the donors give."

"You've made a big jump from executive with all the perks to running the mill. Are you really ready to leave all this behind?"

He looked around the room, seeing so many people he knew, so much from the life he'd built away from Blackstone Manor. "My family, brothers, Carter—" *You.* "Sometimes life is where you're needed. Besides, I won't be giving it up completely."

He felt her stiffen beneath his fingers. "What do you mean?" she asked, her voice calm despite her body's message.

"I've enjoyed working with this children's charity for a good many years. While I won't be located in the city, I will be visiting regularly and remain on the board to help keep it viable." He smiled down at her. "I think we'll have plenty of opportunities for glamour, because I'd sure hate to never see you in this dress again."

Her husky laugh tingled along his nerves. "You are such a man," she said.

He couldn't resist this time. His hips pressed briefly

against her before he returned to a polite distance. "Yes, ma'am, I certainly am."

She tightened her grip as if she would pull him back to her, but she, too, continued the proper dance moves. The decorum of their public display only emphasized to him exactly what was lurking beneath the surface. Fire and need that burned so much hotter for their restraint. He struggled to concentrate.

"I've thought of establishing some kind of foundation in Black Hills," he said, his shaky control letting his private thoughts free. "I simply haven't found a cause that's spoken to me quite yet."

"It should be one you feel passionate about," she said, licking her lips in such a way that he knew she was talking about something else, something far more private.

"I know," he said, struggling to rein in his control. Since he couldn't have her body, he let his mind wander and kept talking. "Here, a job is a job. In Black Hills, my job is about more—it's about keeping a community alive and protecting a way of life. Not as a monument to my grandfather but to something—" Jacob wasn't sure how to articulate the emotions swirling through him.

"What?" KC asked, her voice husky, her eyes searching for the truth.

He couldn't help giving it to her. "Something that means more than a dollar amount, something my son—" he swallowed hard "—and you can be proud of."

He felt her hands clutch against him once more, but she didn't speak for a moment. "Having a kid changes a lot about your perspective, doesn't it?"

"Uncomfortably so," Jacob admitted with a quiet laugh, grateful for a break in the emotional tension building between them. "But all these charity events have taught me one thing," he added, pulling her just a touch closer so his body took control of the dance in an elemental way.

"What's that?"

"I dance a heck of a lot better than I did in high school." And he swirled her around the floor, expertly leading her around other couples to end with a flourish as the music crescendoed. He tipped her back, savoring the slide of her hips against his as he pulled her gently up into his arms. This time he didn't hold back. Despite the crowded room, he let his lips find hers and do the rest of the talking.

"Let's leave," KC murmured against his lips. Her body couldn't seem to break the contact. "I've waited long enough."

Even in the dim light KC could see the *yes* that leaped to Jacob's face, though he managed to maintain a strained outer decorum. He immediately ushered her across the crowded room toward the exit. Laughter bubbled up at his quick pace, but she wasn't about to argue. The door was just in sight when a man stepped into their path.

He stuck out his hand with a grin, completely unaware of his unwelcome intrusion. "Jacob, wonderful event. I hope there will be many more, despite you leaving us…"

To anyone else, Jacob's switch to consummate gentleman would have appeared seamless. Only KC noticed the tightness of his stance and the tick of the muscle in his cheek as he introduced Robert and his wife, Vanessa. The Williamsons had been to many of these events with Jacob, since Robert also served on the board of the charity.

As they chatted around her, KC almost felt bad about knowingly pushing Jacob past his limits today in an attempt to make her point. But she had a feeling the wait would be worth it. She shivered, drawing Jacob's arm around her bare shoulders as he spoke. Today had been a day outside of her normal experience with men, or even with Jacob. Funny, serious, sexy, emotional. If this kept up, she'd be treading some dangerous waters.

The men chatted about some project they had worked on together, giving KC a clue that this could take a few minutes. So she turned to Vanessa. "How are you tonight?" she asked politely.

Vanessa's smile was slightly off-kilter, just a little too wide to be completely natural. "Oh, just fine," she said with a heavy Southern drawl. "Where are you from?"

KC relaxed a little. "I'm from Black Hills, South Carolina."

"So Jacob finally got him a down-home girl. Guess that's what's keeping him entertained in the back of beyond."

KC raised her brows, a little taken aback, even though the woman's tone hadn't been ugly. She was even more surprised as Vanessa looped her arm through hers. "Let's have a little chat and a drink. I could most definitely use another."

Of coffee. KC had dealt with enough drinkers to know that Vanessa was a couple of drinks away from having to be carried home. Or embarrassing herself and her husband.

They settled at the bar, and Vanessa ordered a martini. "Sparkling water with lemon for me," KC said.

Vanessa didn't seem to notice. They chatted about the party for a moment—the gorgeous decorations, delicious desserts and cool little band—before Vanessa asked, "So what do you do?"

It seemed that KC didn't have the appearance of a woman of leisure. "I'm a bartender."

Vanessa looked at her with surprise, and then their bartender set their drinks in front of them. Without missing a beat, KC switched the glasses, setting the water firmly in front of Vanessa.

"Hey, that's mine," she said with a frown.

"You don't really need it, do you?"

Vanessa stiffened. "I'm not drunk."

As all tipsy people insisted… "I didn't say you were," KC said, adopting the reasonable tone she knew would work with someone of Vanessa's personality. "But do you really want to end the night puking on those fabulous Jimmy Choo shoes?"

Vanessa blinked at her for a moment, then her eyes watered. She quickly glanced down at her shoes. "You have a point."

Good. Vanessa seemed nice, straightforward and interested in her as a person, not just as Jacob's date. KC would hate to see her move into obnoxious territory. Besides, her people radar made her wonder if there was something else going on here.

Vanessa tipped her water glass at KC before taking a long drink. Then she gave a half smile. "Well, I'm betting you're a good bartender," she conceded. "Is that how you met Jacob? In the bar?"

"Nope. I met him on a plane. I'm not the best flyer."

"That's a shame," Vanessa said.

Confused, KC asked, "Why?"

"Because being in a bar would mean Jacob was having some fun. He needs to have a good time every once in a while. He's so serious, as if he has something to prove all the time."

"Yes. He does seem that way..." Except in bed. Then his only goal was how many times he could make her explode.

As if she was echoing KC's thoughts, Vanessa leaned closer and asked, "Is he that focused in bed? Bet he would view each woman as a challenge to be solved."

Um... "I hope that's the alcohol talking."

"Nope," Vanessa said with a saucy grin, the alcoholic haze starting to fade from her movements. "I'm just too curious for my own good—especially about hunks all hidden under the perfect business suit."

KC had dealt with a lot of unexpected conversations, but this one truly caught her off guard. At least Vanessa was still curious, which meant she didn't know for sure. Still, KC wasn't comfortable engaging in traditional girl talk with a stranger. Not that she was ready to talk about

Jake at all in that capacity—it was too new, too intimate, too complicated…

"Not gonna say? I don't blame you," Vanessa conceded. She shook her empty glass at the bartender for a refill. "I'm happy for him. Although having him move permanently because he's finally found something to take his mind off work will deplete the eye candy around Philadelphia."

KC just raised her brows. Vanessa had obviously said what she wanted; maybe that was just the alcohol. But at least she was up-front and friendly about it.

And she wasn't done. "You're lucky," Vanessa said with a frown into her now-full glass of lemon water. "My husband has hardly looked at me all night."

Ah, now this situation was making more sense. KC jumped in headfirst, since Vanessa seemed the type to appreciate straight talk. "Have you made him look at you instead of wasting your time drinking?"

Vanessa stilled for a moment.

"I know we just met, but you don't seem like a woman who takes no for an answer," KC said, spotting the men approaching over Vanessa's shoulder. "So don't give him the chance to ignore you. You deserve better."

"Everything okay, ladies?" Robert asked as he reached his wife's side. He studied her glass for a moment.

"We're good," Vanessa said, winking in KC's direction. "But I'm in serious need of a dance with my husband."

Robert nodded, but his attention had already been snagged by a passing suit. "Yes, dear, I just need to see—"

"No, Robert," Vanessa interrupted as she regained her feet. Not a wobble in sight, despite her four-inch heels. "You can talk *after*. This sexy getup shouldn't go to waste." She paused, giving her husband a chance to look for himself—and he did.

KC suppressed a grin. Sometimes changing a man's focus was way too easy.

Without further interruption, Vanessa led her husband

to the dance floor, Robert's focus definitely where it should be. Vanessa threw a wink KC's way as she slid confidently into his arms.

Jacob glanced between them suspiciously, then shook his head with a grin. "I don't want to know," he said.

He pressed a kiss to her neck, eliciting a shiver. Then he whispered, "Where were we?"

He had her out the door and hailing a cab before she could answer. Not that she complained. The anticipation of the day had set her senses on high alert. Now she would cap off this romantic night in the perfect way with the man she loved.

KC's stomach dropped as if she'd jump-started an elevator. She'd known she was infatuated with Jacob, but she thought she'd been able to wall off all those tender feelings, leaving only the attraction. Seeing so many different sides to him over the past month had only deepened her desire for something more, some permanent attachment to this strong, steady man.

She had no doubt he would never turn away from Carter, but his son was his blood. He'd turned his life upside down in recent months to help his family. But she wasn't family… She was expendable.

The one thing she'd always feared.

She had been determined to be the strong one, the one who could walk away. And she had, but she couldn't stay gone. Would she survive if he chose to leave her?

KC forced herself to shut down her thoughts as Jacob led her into the bedroom of their suite. The moonlight streaming through the gauzy curtains glinted off his blond hair as he peeled himself out of the black jacket of his tux. He unbuttoned his dress shirt, revealing his muscled chest a few inches at a time.

He pulled the ends of the shirt from his pants, leaving it to hang open as he stalked closer to her. Half sophisticate, half primal male. KC's heart fluttered in feminine awareness. She backed slowly away.

Jake kept coming, his intense stare telling her everything he would enjoy doing to her. But first…

"I've been dreaming about what's underneath this dress since this afternoon, KC," he said, his deep voice brushing along her senses with the skill of a master musician. "Now I will see it for myself."

She smiled up at him. "That was the plan."

Reaching to the side, Jacob eased her zipper down until the unique creation slid to the floor, leaving her more vulnerable and exposed than she'd ever been. Not because the corset left little to the imagination with its mesh panels, but because the man before her wasn't looking for a good time—he was intent on consuming her.

And she would let him.

His palms traced the boning from her hips up to her waist, then around to her plump breasts beneath the satin cups. The flesh swelled, threatening to overflow its bounds. "KC," Jake said, sounding a little strangled. "White satin. Couldn't be more appropriate for my angel."

She didn't know why he was comparing her to a heavenly being, but she'd savor the reverence in his voice, his touch. He continued to explore, running his hands back down to the garters attached to her stockings, then up the back to the completely unprotected roundness of her backside. With a firm grip, he pulled her against him. The friction of his tuxedo pants and the stockings on her legs sent her head spinning. Her hands dipped beneath his shirttails, meeting warm flesh just above his belt. Part of her ached for more; part of her reveled in the joyous miracle of having Jake in full flesh before her.

Only this close could she feel the slight tremble in his muscles, feel the sheer sheen of sweat over his skin.

"KC," he said with a groan. "I wanted to wait, honey. To make it last. But I can't."

"Then take me, Jake," she whispered against his skin. "Take all of me."

Two steps and he had her balanced on the edge of the dresser, knees spread wide to accommodate him. His touch was rough this time as he dragged the cups of the bustier down to give him full access to the treasure he sought.

Her heart raced into overdrive as his mouth teased her nipples. Then he gave a soft pull that strengthened the pulse that beat between her thighs. She needed him…needed him…

He didn't disappoint.

Seconds later he was pushing inside her, filling her in the best way imaginable. Physically, emotionally. Stretching her to accept him. Overwhelming her protests. Completing her in a way she'd never thought possible.

His mouth settled at her neck, sucking along her skin. His thumb pressed against that most precious of spots as she panted out her need. All the while, the hard strokes from his body drove her insane until all the sensations coalesced into a crescendo of heat that detonated in a single blinding second. Jake's hoarse cries in her ear pulled her back from heavenly nothingness to the precious gift of his own release.

They drifted back to reality together, aftershocks rocking them for long, long moments. Then he tried to pull away—and stumbled. Shocked, she clutched at him.

Beneath her fingers, a rumble started, then grew into laughter. Jake's laughter was that much more precious for being so rare. "What's so funny?" she asked.

"My pants are still around my ankles," he confessed.

She couldn't help it. She had to laugh, too. "Well, let's get you properly undressed before you fall and we have to spend the evening in the emergency room rather than the bedroom."

He was already stripping himself down. "Yes, ma'am. That sounds like a perfect plan to me."

Twelve

The ringing of the phone roused KC from the deepest sleep she'd ever had. At least, it felt that way. Maybe because she'd so rarely gotten a full night's sleep since Carter was born—

Carter!

KC was standing next to the bed before she even realized she'd moved. Her vision blurred for a moment before she blinked, her body swaying in confusion. Who was she kidding? It was always hard to wake up.

With deliberate focus, she found Jacob sitting on the bed with his back to her, phone to his ear. Had his movement woken her or the phone? Confusion once more clouded her mind for a moment until he stood and ended the call.

"Get dressed," Jacob said, clipped and to the point. "We need to go."

Carter?

Concentration was hard to come by, but KC forced herself to snap to it. By then, the passionate, compelling lover of last night had been replaced by a man in full action mode. Jacob was already dressed in cargo pants and a casual polo for traveling. He swept out the bedroom door with his phone, leaving her on her own.

With the urgency of a worried mother, she quickly followed him. “Is Carter all right?”

Jacob didn’t answer. She moved around the couch to see his phone in his hands, his fingers speeding across the screen.

“Jacob, what’s wrong?”

Still no answer. Anger swept through her this time. His focus was so intent that she got close without him even noticing. She reached out her hand and covered the phone so he couldn’t see it.

He glanced up, frowning in her direction.

“Is Carter okay?” she asked, enunciating each word.

He blinked, and she could almost see the realization steal into his eyes. *Yes, dear, you left something out.* “I’m sorry, KC. Yes, Carter is perfectly fine.”

“Then what’s wrong?”

“Just something out at the mill,” he said, but his normally straightforward gaze slid away. He stepped back, dropping the phone to his side. “But I really need to be on the next flight home.”

What was going on? Why was Jacob avoiding the issue with her? Or was he so focused on what was happening back home that his mind had already traveled there, leaving her behind? She returned to the bedroom to dress and pack, but her thoughts lingered on the man who was already back furiously texting once more. After last night, she would have described them as being closer than ever.

So why had he pulled away?

As they left the hotel, her heart mourned the short duration of their time alone together. They were supposed to have been here for two more days, but whatever was going on at the mill was important enough to cut their visit short. The delicious ache between her thighs reminded her just what she was forfeiting. But it had to be bad for Jacob to need to be home so quickly, didn’t it? Hopefully everyone was all right.

Not that Jacob was talking. She finally closed her eyes on the plane and attempted to make up for the lack of sleep the previous night. Jacob's restlessness beside her kept her from more than dozing, but at least she got some rest and felt better able to handle an afternoon alone with Carter. Obviously Jacob wouldn't be there to help.

"I'll take you to your mother's to get Carter, then I'll need to head out for a while," he said as they collected the car from long-term parking. "There are some things I need to check into with Aiden."

Not wanting to pry but hating the timidness of her question, she asked, "Is there anything I can do to help?"

A sharp shake of his head was the only answer. His silence frustrated her, but she refused to beg. So she backed off after that, spending the rest of the ride to town in silence. As long as her son was okay, she could handle anything else.

Or so she thought.

As they neared Lola's, the space between the bar's parking lot and her mother's small house was occupied with a couple of city police cars and a whole crowd of people. Fear pounded inside KC's chest as if she was having a heart attack. Instead of stopping, Jacob accelerated past the building.

"What? Wait!"

Confusion and panic had her twisting in her seat. Jacob parked on the side of the road a little way down. "I thought you said Carter was okay," KC gasped. Jacob barely had time to stop the car before she had her door open and was running for the house.

It wasn't until she started pushing through the crowd that she realized Jacob wasn't with her. She glanced back over her shoulder and saw him slowly approaching, but then she broke through to the other side of the crowd and her thoughts were only for her family.

As she mounted the first step to the porch, the door

opened and a few of the local deputies she recognized from the bar came out. Surprise jolted through her as her brother appeared between them. Faces grim, they all crossed the porch together and filed down the steps. Murmuring from the crowd behind her swelled, but she only had eyes for Zachary. One of the officers had his hands on Zachary's arm, which told her he wasn't just going for a joyride.

"Zachary?" she called, but somehow Jacob was there, holding her out of the way of the approaching party.

The deputy escorting her brother paused, giving her a better look. No handcuffs. "Zachary," she whispered, fear double-timing her pulse.

"It's okay, KC," her brother said, his face carefully unconcerned. "Everything will be fine."

But she didn't believe him. Especially when they escorted him to a cop car and into the backseat. Jacob remained silent the whole time. Behind her, the screen door banged. Turning, KC found her mother on the porch. "Mom?" KC's voice broke as she rushed up the steps, Jacob finally letting her go.

"They said something about some crops he dusted last week," her mother murmured, her eyes glued to the cop cars backing out of the driveway. "Said they're dying or something. They had lots of questions for him."

KC turned accusing eyes on Jacob. She could read his knowledge of the situation in his body language. He'd known. And hadn't told her.

As if he could read her body language, too, Jacob said, "KC, I'm sorry. I didn't know they'd be here. I thought they'd pick him up at his apartment."

"He was here helping me fix the sink," KC's mom said. "It was clogged. I guess his landlord told them where to find him."

"What's going to happen?" KC asked.

Jacob slowly shook his head, his eyes once more guarded. He glanced at the people behind him. The crowd was diminishing, but those remaining seemed very interested in KC and Jacob's presence. "Let's get you and Carter home. Quietly. You can rest while I look into it."

But he knew more than he was saying. More than he would share. Which proved to KC that there was something important going on—but he wasn't going to include her.

"Don't bother," she said, taking a step back up toward the porch. "Mom will get me home."

Even though she wanted to believe he had a reason for his actions, nothing hurt worse than his turning and walking away—without a word.

"Your sister is going to come after me with a cast-iron skillet if I don't come home with the right answers soon," Jacob said to the man sitting across from him in the local police station's tiny interrogation room.

Not to mention that I'll be back to sleeping on the couch tonight.

Zachary smirked as if he could read Jacob's mind. "Well, you're the one who played mute. Why didn't you just tell her what was going on? Trust me, KC can take it."

Obviously a lot better than Jacob. He hadn't known what to say or how to say it, so he'd said nothing. He'd let his business mode take over, oblivious to KC's need to know.

Plus, the crowd had made him nervous. Who knew if the saboteur was watching, enjoying the drama, waiting for Zachary to be charged with a crime he didn't commit? At least intentionally. Or had he?

This situation was majorly screwed up. So Jacob had remained silent. Something he just knew KC would make him pay for, with relish.

"Just tell me again what happened," he said, hoping to block that out for a few more minutes.

Luckily the local police knew Jacob, had been working with him and Aiden and management to try to catch whoever was sabotaging things at the mill. He also saw the sheriff a couple of times a month at the local country club, so they'd let him in to see Zachary, who wasn't technically under arrest…yet.

"After my army gig, I missed flying, so I bought a little Cessna to do some crop-dusting work during the growing and harvest seasons. People like me because I do good work and am reasonably priced, so almost ninety percent of the farmers around here use me."

Zachary rubbed his hand over his shaggy black hair. "A few days ago I took the plane out to dust pesticides over a lot of the cotton crops in the area. Did the rest of my customers the next day. Well, apparently those crops have started dying. All of them."

Jacob sucked in a breath and held it for a moment, then let it out in a rush. "How bad?"

Zachary's green-brown eyes, so like his sister's, met Jacob's. "If all of them die…? We're talking total devastation for this community. I think all of those farms sell to the mill, so you'll have practically no raw material come harvesttime." Zachary's fists clenched. "Not to mention the number of families who no longer have cash for their crops this year. How could somebody do this?"

"So you didn't do it?"

Once more Zachary's gaze met his. "Oh, I did it. I flew the plane. But I have no idea how I could have dumped something that would kill the plants. When I loaded, those tanks were marked for common pesticides."

"Tell me what happened from the moment you arrived at the airfield."

He knew Zachary had to be tired of repeating the story, but Jacob had to be sure the man was telling the truth. For himself and the company. But most of all for KC.

But Zachary didn't falter as he related step by step how he checked in, confirmed and loaded the tanks and prepared for takeoff. Behind him, the deputy nodded. Seemed as if Zachary was telling the truth.

"Why would someone want to do this?" Zachary demanded. "And why through me? I hate that."

Jacob sympathized with Zachary's anger. And admired his calm. After all, he was sitting in a police station. The deputy had said, depending on what happened, he could be facing destruction-of-property charges for every family that had been harmed. That was a lot of charges.

Hopefully, Jacob could prevent that.

"What do you think was used?"

Zachary shrugged, his palms opening in a "how should I know" gesture. "Honestly, I haven't seen any of the plants, so I'm not sure. The chemical tests will tell them what they need to know."

The door opened and the local police chief walked in with Aiden. The police chief spoke first, confirming that they'd been listening through the speakers. "We've sent samples off, but it will take a while for them to come back."

"I loaded the right tanks," Zachary insisted. "I double-checked myself."

Aiden jumped in, his narrowed gaze not leaving Zachary for a second. "Look, I don't know anything about farming. That's not a secret. But something wiped out those plants, and a lot of livelihoods with it."

"One of the deputies on the scene confirmed that the tanks are marked and were checked into inventory as pesticides," the police chief said. "Not that it would stop someone from putting something else inside them."

Jacob found himself defending Zachary, even though Aiden was clearly suspicious. "Why would he kill plants and his own income with them?" he asked.

Zachary snorted. "Damn straight. Shut down the mill, the farmers and my own earnings in the process."

Aiden nodded. "Makes sense."

Jacob could see his brother mulling it over as he started to pace. It did make sense as a defense. But would it be enough?

"Although," Aiden continued, flashing a concerned look in Jacob's direction, "if you were paid to do this, it would be a lot more than the income you normally make."

Zachary dropped his head into his hands.

The chief answered his phone, spoke quietly for a few moments, then ended the call. "After examining a sample of the crops, the consensus seems to be they were sprayed with defoliant."

Silence reigned for a moment. Zachary's head dropped into his hands. "At this early stage, that means death for all those plants."

The deputy nodded. "Most likely."

"Jeez."

Jacob shared a look with Aiden. Not good. But then Aiden surprised him. "How accessible are the tanks to somebody besides yourself?"

"I guess someone could get to them," Zachary said with a frown, "even though they're locked up. And of course, some of the airport security personnel have the key."

"It's a small facility," the policeman said, "and a lot of locals hang out there. Especially the older men. So a good bunch of people come and go without much notice. Someone dropping by wouldn't stand out too much."

Zachary's eyes met Jacob's, letting him know their thoughts matched. Their saboteur had expanded his reach.

"How long does he need to stay here?" Jacob asked.

"A few hours," the chief said. "Then he can go. For now."

Zachary groaned.

The chief shot him a sympathetic look. "Sorry, son, but I can't make any guarantees until I get to the bottom of this. Which we will. I promise."

Zachary looked more defeated than he had since Jacob had arrived. Not that he could blame him. After all, he had sprayed the plants. But did that mean he was responsible for the destruction if he'd sprayed the defoliant unknowingly?

"Look at it this way," Jacob said in a lighter tone.

"Wouldn't you rather be here than having to explain this to your sister? Like I'm going to have to do?"

Because Jacob had no doubt his girl would be ready for a come-to-Jesus meeting when he got home. He'd better have some answers, or his head would be on a skewer.

Thirteen

Jacob opened the door quietly, anxious not to wake Carter. It was long past the time he should have been home. Worried about Zachary and how what had happened would affect the town, he'd hung around until Zachary was released. Then he, Zachary and Aiden had spent some time going over all the information they had. Jacob had texted KC when Zachary had left jail, but hadn't talked to her since then.

One look at KC's face and he realized it was a whole lot worse than he'd anticipated. She gently jiggled and rocked the restless baby in her arms, but her red-rimmed eyes and flushed cheeks attested to how upset she was. And to Jacob's guilt. He still found her disheveled look cute, but he knew better than to say so.

Carter seemed to sense his mother's unhappiness. There was no full-blown crying this time, just a restless stirring of arms and legs to keep himself awake. Without a word, Jacob lifted Carter from her arms and tucked him into his own special hold. His son looked up at him long and hard, then blinked slowly. Once. Then again. And started his slow slide into sleep as Jacob swayed him back and forth.

As those incredible eyes closed for a final time, Jacob

smiled. "He seems to have grown in just the small amount of time we've been gone."

KC nodded, though she kept her face averted after his one quick glimpse. "Yeah, incredible, huh?"

He winced at her scratchy voice, feeling himself falling into unknown depths. The KC he knew was strong, independent, sexy. He'd never seen her cry. That was something he truly didn't know how to handle. To escape, he carried Carter down the hall to his room and settled him into bed. Staring into the crib, he took several deep breaths before going back down the hallway.

Jacob couldn't leave her hurting. The woman he cared for deserved better than that. So he found her at the sink, washing bottles. He suspected it was simply an excuse to hide her face from him, but he would allow her that modicum of privacy. It was the least he could do after telling her nothing, rushing her home and then leaving her with Carter by herself all night.

"I waited until they released him, just in case. Then he, Aiden and I went over everything together. I didn't mean to be so long."

"Do you suspect him?"

"Zachary? Once I heard all the facts? No."

She turned to face him, her stare demanding in its own right. "Tell me the truth, Jacob."

"KC, Zach is not the saboteur." He held her gaze, intent on conveying his belief. "I know because I've asked him to help me catch whoever is doing all this."

Her face completely blanked for a moment. "What?"

"Your brother works maintenance at the mill. He's all over the floor, sometimes at odd hours, and no one thinks anything of him being there. He's been keeping his eyes and ears open for me. That may be why he was targeted this way."

With deliberate intent, he stepped closer. "That's why I didn't say anything while the police were picking him up at your mother's. I wasn't sure who might be watching, listening in that crowd, and I certainly didn't want your mother to think I'd put Zach in this position."

"I—"

He'd never seen her this much at a loss for words.

"Jacob, I don't even know what to say."

"Zachary will be fine."

"This isn't about Zachary." Her voice gained volume until Jacob worried about waking Carter. "I can't believe you don't see that. This has nothing to do with my brother, and everything to do with you not keeping me in the loop."

Jacob stared for a moment. She was right—he hadn't seen that as the real problem, more as a sideline. Jacob proceeded with caution. "I didn't think you cared about the day-to-day stuff at the mill."

"This isn't a daily occurrence, is it? You said you were worried about my and Carter's safety, but you don't even let me know you've put my brother in a position that could get him hurt, or even just fired?"

Well, no. That was definitely not the right answer. "I thought I was approaching the situation logically. I needed help—"

"A spy."

"—and your brother agreed to help me. It's business, not personal."

"When it involves my family, I consider everything personal."

Huh. Jacob wasn't even sure how to respond to that. He knew KC approached things emotionally, but he hadn't thought this would ever come up. He had never imagined the saboteur would use Zachary to hurt the mill.

She didn't comment on his silence. "Why is it okay to keep us in the dark and let us think he's going to jail for something we know he would never do? My mother has been calling me, worried sick. I've been worried. When you don't let me know what's going on, what am I supposed to think?"

"I told you I'd take care of him. Zach won't go to jail. I promise. We've got a plan."

She turned that heartbreaking gaze on him full force. "But I'm not part of it, am I?"

No. It had never occurred to him that she'd want to be, even though he knew how much she loved her family. He felt like such an idiot.

"I don't expect you to hire me so I can watch my brother at work. Or text me a minute-by-minute update. But I'm not some old-fashioned maiden who sits home by the fire while you do all the work. I thought you knew me better than that. It has to be more than just a text here and there. If we're—if we are going to be partners, I need you to include me, accept me as part of the plan. Keep me informed ahead of time, not after the fact. That's what partners do."

Jacob wasn't sure if he could promise that. He cared about her. He knew that. But he'd been doing this on his own for so long. He didn't know if he could open himself up to the idea of partners, especially one that operated so differently from him.

He wanted KC to trust him. Even now, he could see the fear cloud her eyes. But working on his own terms was what he knew. Could he change that?

"I need you to decide, Jacob. Are we working together, or are you strictly solo?"

His only answer was to pull her close and hold on tight. He couldn't bring himself to lie, so he kept his fears locked inside. The only truth he knew was that the man he was now would die if she left him all alone.

Zachary let out a low whistle as Jacob led him into the breezeway at the heart of Blackstone Manor. "Wow. And I thought this place was impressive from the outside."

Jacob let him look his fill around the central corridor

and the staircase, which gave visitors an unobstructed view of the elaborate railings on the landings of the two upper floors.

"At least now it's seeing some true happiness," a feminine voice said.

Jacob smiled up at his sister-in-law, Christina, as she descended from the second floor. Her lilac scrubs contrasted with the dark waves of hair falling to her shoulders. "How's Mother?" he asked.

Christina gave a sad little smile. "The same. Today's a pretty good day for her." She turned to the other visitor. "Hey, Zachary. How are you?"

"Good for now," he returned with a grin. "The police confirmed that there's no proof I added the defoliant to the tank, which was marked pesticide. But the two working security cameras were turned off that night, so I'm still the primary suspect, mostly because I'm the *only* suspect. But my guess is, they're also waiting to see if any money turns up."

Jacob watched as the two chatted. He'd known Christina and KC were friends but didn't realize Christina knew Zach. It shouldn't surprise him, though. Christina had a knack for connecting with people that Jacob had always envied.

"How is KC?" Christina asked. "I haven't seen her in several days."

"She's been subdued when I've seen her at Lola's," Zachary said. "Hovering over me like I might disappear at any moment, though they've been keeping me mostly in the back to discourage any retaliation. She's worried about the farmers."

So was Jacob, but he hadn't figured out what to do yet. "She's quiet at home, too."

Another situation Jacob didn't know how to fix. Jacob knew he hadn't convinced her of his loyalty, or his desire to be equal partners. Taking the steps to truly include her in every part of his life had his control-freak side, well, freaking out. So they danced around each other, keeping every conversation light, not delving too deep into things that might be tricky to navigate. Then at night, after Carter was asleep, their bodies talked intimately in a whole different language.

"Oh, Jacob's got that 'worried about my woman' look," Christina said with a grin. "I think he's doomed. What do you think, Zachary?"

"I'm pretty sure you're right." Zachary gave him a speculative once-over, but in the end nodded his approval. "She could do worse."

Jacob did not want to get into this. He looked expectantly at Christina. "Aiden?"

Her smirk told him she knew his avoidance tactics well, but she let him slide. "He's in the study."

Jacob led the way around the staircase and halfway down the breezeway until he came to his grandfather's former study. Zachary's expression said *wow* as he took in the floor-to-ceiling scrollwork bookcases and masculine furnishings.

Aiden greeted them with a distracted nod. "He's gone off campus again."

Jacob shook his head at Zachary. "For some reason, he thinks we can read his mind. Do you mean the saboteur, Aiden?"

His brother frowned. "You know I do, Jacob."

"The fact that he's hitting places away from the plant worries me," Jacob said. "It makes him—or them—dangerous."

"And unpredictable," Zachary added.

"Messing with things around the mill itself is annoying and a concern. But no one has been hurt on mill property. But showing that he's willing to expand his targets outside the mill itself? This convinces me that whoever was behind this incident was behind the group who set fire to my studio," Aiden said, his steely gaze meeting Jacob's.

His heart skipped a beat. That meant KC could still become a target…or an innocent bystander who got in the way. "I'm doing what I can to keep them safe."

Always observant, Zachary didn't miss the subtext. "Is this why you're still keeping your attachment to my sister on the down low?"

KC's brother deserved the truth, and giving him the information would mean that there'd be one more person to watch over Jacob's new family. "It's not the only reason, but yes, I don't want KC and Carter to become targets, so we're being careful to keep things casual in public."

The look Zachary threw his way made Jacob think he wanted to know the other reasons, but Jacob didn't want to talk about the deal he'd forced Zachary's sister into playing out.

"Zachary," Aiden said, averting his attention from Jacob, "what are you hearing at the plant?"

"Well, there's lots to hear," he said with a slow shake of his head. "Rumblings all over the floor. Low level up to management. And I mean a lot. Mostly upset over whoever did this, but—"

He paused, his face taking on an uncomfortable look.

"What is it?" Jacob asked.

"There're also people talking down on management for not putting a stop to the sabotage by now. People worried they'll be the next target. Or simply get in the way and get hurt." He steeled his hands against his hips. "A lot of people know those farmers, their relatives, friends. I can see the situation escalating. Soon. But I'll never know about anything before it happens."

"Why?" Jacob asked.

"I'm persona non grata right now. By association, you know."

"How hard is this hitting the farmers?" Aiden asked.

"Some of them have day jobs, so that helps, but without a crop to harvest, that guaranteed income won't be there. They'll lose their investment. Some years, their income might fluctuate if the season is too wet or too dry, but this is a complete wipeout. Bad is an understatement."

Jacob was ready for action. "What do they need? Money? Food? What would be best?"

"It's probably different for different people," Aiden said. "Let's think on it. Zachary, you get back to us if you find out more."

"I already know one thing you're gonna need."

"What's that?" Aiden asked.

"Cotton." Zachary paused a moment, as if letting that soak in. "We've got to find a cotton dealer—soon. KC might can help you with that. She's got a good friend who's a cotton dealer. Works with some of the farmers around here, too."

Involve KC? Jacob's first instinct was to keep her out of this. There were people at the plant who could handle it. But Jacob felt a personal responsibility for the farmers and the people at the mill, and wanted to fix things himself. And this just might be his chance to prove to KC that he was willing to include her in this decision. That they were in this together.

Fourteen

Jacob watched KC finish washing up behind the bar. Normally, when it was past closing time, he would have already left, taken Carter home and put him to bed so she didn't have to do that after a long shift on her feet. But her mother had asked if Carter could spend the night. Jacob's standing with her was still precarious; she'd given him a stern look before nodding in her daughter's direction, as if to say *fix this.*

KC had been unnaturally subdued since the police had interviewed Zachary. He wasn't used to this. Normally, her every movement, no matter how quiet, was filled with life. Now she seemed to spend her days on Pause, as if her spirit were holding its breath, waiting to see what was going to happen next.

An even bigger problem: Jacob wasn't sure if she was worried about Zachary…or the two of them.

Tonight, he needed a chance to reconnect with her. Not just sexually. KC was open to his touch, but even there he could feel her holding herself away from him. Not losing herself quite as fully as she normally did in their passion. Which hurt. Ms. Gatlin's offer to take Carter for the night provided the perfect opportunity to fix things.

KC's mother left with Carter, who was already falling asleep in her arms. Still, KC kept scrubbing.

Jacob moved to a spot directly across the bar from her, but she didn't look up. Finally he reached out and stilled her hand with his own. "KC, I need your help."

Now he had her attention. *Such a mama bear.* "What's wrong?"

"The farmers and their families are going to need support to get back on their feet. I'm trying to figure out the best way to do that."

"Another fund-raiser?"

Jacob shook his head. "No, I was thinking something more personal. First, I need a cotton dealer, or a lot of people are gonna be out of a job come September. Zachary said you could help."

She paused in her scrubbing, those turbulent eyes suddenly lighting up. "Easy peasy."

Was she being glib? "Really?"

"Yep. I know exactly who to contact." She grinned, her first genuine smile in days. "A guy I met when he first started working with the farmers out here about five years ago. He doesn't buy in Black Hills every year, but he keeps track of sales around here." She dropped her rag into the dishwater, giving Jacob her full attention. "What else?"

"A lot of people lost their immediate livelihood. They're going to have some tangible needs. Remember me telling you that I wanted to invest in a charity that spoke to me?"

KC nodded, her eyes sparking green deep inside the brown.

"This is it, but I want to start off right. I have some ideas, but I'm used to how charities work in a big city." Which was totally true. More than that, he wanted her involved. Soliciting her ideas was the best way to get her on board. "I don't want some anonymous charity run by a big impersonal board. This would be a hands-on project. But I don't have time to run it. Any ideas?"

She propped her elbows on the bar. Resting her chin in her hands gave him a distracting view of her cleavage, but he maintained his focus. Barely. KC appeared oblivious as she said, "Better to be effective than to just do something for the sake of doing it."

Exactly. "I want a hardship fund to provide a variety of things to families and workers in need. But the community as a whole still views me as an outsider, I think. I'm not familiar with the people here nearly enough. And they probably wouldn't feel comfortable with me, either."

He smiled as he continued, "We need someone to administer the fund who is familiar with the townspeople on a grassroots level. That's why I wanted to ask if you would be willing to help me. You know these people. You know this place. Will you do this for them?"

Shock widened her eyes. Her mouth shaped the word *me*, but no sound escaped. A few heartbeats later, she cleared her throat. "Jacob, I don't know anything about coordinating a big charity. I mean, I do know a lot of people—"

"And you know about handling them, evaluating what they need with dignity and respect. Sounds perfect to me. I can manage the boring parts of it—the money and paperwork and all."

She stood quietly for a moment. "What about the saboteur? Do we need to worry about him retaliating against me?"

"For helping the community? I doubt it. He seems more concerned with things that directly affect the mill. The goal has been accomplished—kill the cotton. Helping the people left behind shouldn't endanger you. Now, Aiden and I bringing in cotton could be a trigger."

She squirmed, the light in her eyes dimming a little.

"Don't worry. As long as we're careful to keep our public interactions nonromantic, you and Carter should be fine."

"Maybe." She studied him for a long moment. "You

know people will eventually find out you're living at my house?"

"As I said, we're being careful."

"Yes, and they've stopped questioning your presence here. And the neighbors don't notice your car parked in the back shed. And we're careful not to go anywhere out together. But how long will you be happy with that?"

Her tone told him she wasn't happy, but she was probably too afraid for Carter to push the issue. He wasn't sure how he felt about going public, but he couldn't force himself to leave her—them. One day he might have to, to protect them both. But for now, staying was his only desire. He gave her a short nod, keeping his thoughts to himself. "We'll deal with that when we get there. For now, what about the charity?"

"Um, okay. I mean, yes," she said, then laughed as he nodded his approval.

Now they were on track—and seeing her so excited had an incredibly stimulating effect on his libido. "Any ideas for what we could do?"

"Maybe we could raise money for care packages, get donated gift cards for clothes and groceries, or even money to help pay essential bills."

"Baby, you've got some great ideas in that head of yours."

Resorting to her sexy persona, Miss Mischievous winked at him. "Sure you don't want a fund-raiser? I could open a kissing booth."

Unable to stop himself, he grasped her hand. "I don't think so, woman," he said, the deeply possessive note betraying him, but he didn't care. "The only man kissing you will be me."

"Ooh, territorial." The heat filling her eyes belied her light tone.

He rubbed his thumb back and forth over the delicate bones in her hand. "You like?"

"Definitely." Her eyes, green in the dim light, were tentative and fearful as they met his. How could he resist her? As he marched around the bar, her breathing sped up, light and fast.

Jacob used his height to trap her between him and the bar. Need rose like a tsunami, threatening to overwhelm him. "What about this?"

The dilation of her pupils gave him his answer, but he waited for her words. Her permission. "Oh, yeah."

Then he crowded in close, grateful the doors were closed and locked, the lights low or off. Her body felt incredible—muscled legs against his, soft belly cradling his need, full breasts against his ribs. So delectable. So *his.*

He brooked no argument as he pulled her Lola's T-shirt from her jeans and over her head. The low lights glittered off the shimmery satin of the pale pink bra that did a fine job of displaying her womanhood. Unwilling to wait, he lifted her to sit on the counter.

Her squeal of surprise echoed around the empty room, bringing a smile to his lips. *That's right.* He had a few tricks up his sleeve, too. Then he lost himself in the plump upper curve of her silky flesh, kissing his way across the hills and nuzzling into the valley between. He lifted her breasts upward for the return journey, squeezing a little as he dipped his tongue beneath the edge of her bra for a lingering taste of her oh-so-sensitive nipples.

She squirmed and a little whimper escaped her. *Yes, that's what you like.* The way her body went wild under his mouth confirmed it. Her hands clutched at his shoulders, seemingly desperate to drag his clothes off, too, but he wasn't giving in that easy. Instead, he released the clasp that held her bra in place. His hands eased it down her arms to encircle her wrists, then inexorably guided her back until her spine met cold, polished wood. She hissed as she arched up, then moaned once more.

But she wasn't getting away. Control was his. Making her feel him was his only goal.

He palmed his way down her ribs to her waist, then applied his nails to the denim along the inside of her thighs. Her hips lifted, telling him she was willing and ready. Anchoring her hips with his hands, he kissed and nipped lightly, making his way down her body, closer and closer to her core.

"Jake, please," she pleaded, the sound shooting straight to his groin.

"Please what?"

When she didn't answer, he opted for more torture. Reaching under her, he squeezed the ass that had tempted him all evening as she worked the bar, then kissed the bare skin right above the waistband of her jeans.

"Please, Jake," she repeated, her hips lifting for more.

Please what, baby? Jacob waited her out, needing her desperate, aching for him and only him. Sliding his hands up and around, he grasped her waistband and pulled downward as if to remove her jeans.

"Yes," she cried.

"When I say," he growled against her skin, deliberately letting go. She was so beautiful, spread out before him, wanting him. Just as he wanted her.

Her breath panted out, ragged and choppy. Turning the tables, KC dug her fingers into his hair before pulling lightly, eliciting a groan from him. He glanced up and caught the smile stretching her lips. If he'd paid attention to history, he'd have known she wouldn't remain passive for long.

With hands grasping her hips, he pulled her toward him, almost completely shifting her rear off the bar. Her hands slapped against the edge, the sound sharp in the air, as she struggled to keep her balance. He lifted her legs higher, resting them on his shoulders so he could savor the feast before him.

She squeezed, searching for a tighter grip on his shoulders. Her hips lifted higher. Jacob licked his lips, anxious for more, but forced himself to hold back. With sure fingers he unsnapped her jeans. He lingered on the small amount of newly exposed skin for a moment before moving on. This time to the zipper, bringing it down, oh, so slowly.

She moaned her frustration, but he grinned. She was so much fun to play with. His body and mind stilled in surprise for a moment. But yes, he and KC were playing. Not a plan in sight, and it was glorious.

Anxious himself now, he peeled the fabric from her, using her position to keep her helpless and himself in control. Finally, shoes and jeans and panties hit the floor. This time he retraced his journey to her center with sucking kisses and searching tongue.

Before long he couldn't wait himself. He knew to be prepared every second with KC, so he dug the condom out of his pocket and readied himself ASAP. He didn't care that he was almost completely dressed. He needed her now before his body exploded without her.

Together. *Always.*

Jacob couldn't linger on the thought. If he did, he might panic. Lifting her again, he turned and pressed her back against the wall. His weight held her steady while he joined them, her greedy flesh and gasping breaths driving him higher than high. He guided her legs around him and supported her with a hand under each thigh. He started slow, aching to savor, but his body wasn't about to cooperate.

"Jake," she gasped. "Take me, please."

There was his girl. His hips moved with steady purpose, until her breath caught in that familiar way. He leaned down, his head resting against the side of hers. They were so close he could almost hear her heart pound. Only then did he let the emotions take him.

So he shouldn't have been surprised to hear himself whisper the words "I love you" as the world narrowed to the two of them and the ecstasy they found together. KC didn't give any indication that she'd heard him over her gasping cries, but he'd heard. Now he had to decide what to do about it.

When KC said she knew whom to call, she wasn't kidding. Two days after her conversation with Jacob, the cotton agent she had in mind walked into Lola's for a friendly little drink. She'd convinced Jacob to meet him here in a casual atmosphere, rather than having the formal business meeting he'd suggested.

She knew she was right. *Jacob* just didn't know it yet.

"Hey, Toby," she said, grinning at the agent as he slid onto a stool. "How's it going?"

"Always better when I can see your pretty face."

KC laughed at Jacob's glare; he'd approached in time to hear Toby's compliment. Jacob smoothed out his expression as he settled himself onto the stool next to Toby.

"Aw, you're too sweet." She winked, and then motioned to Jacob. "Toby, this is a friend of mine, Jacob Blackstone."

Toby turned an impressed face toward Jacob. "One of the infamous Blackstones? Cool to meet ya, man. I may not have grown up in Black Hills, but everyone in this part of South Carolina has heard of your family."

She could read the minuscule release of tension in Jacob's shoulders as he shook hands with Toby. *Told ya he was cool.* But she just grinned and leaned against the bar.

"I appreciate you dropping by, Toby."

Jacob's gaze dipped down to her chest, reminding her of his attentions on this very bar just a few nights ago. KC quickly straightened up again with a blush.

"Am I gonna get a cherry cola for my trouble?" Toby asked.

"Of course. Want some nachos with that?"

She busied herself making the drink while the guys yakked and got to know each other. Jacob asked about

Toby's hometown, his family, letting him do the talking… and giving KC a chance to watch.

She often watched Jacob surreptitiously while she was working, but today she ached to just soak in his blond good looks. His thick hair feathered back in perfectly clipped waves. Which only made her want to muss them up. She could watch his mouth all day, that tempting curve that gave away all the emotions he tried to keep hidden. Like now. He might be smiling, but she could see the touch of firmness in his lower lip. He was worried about something—probably how this deal would work out. But he'd never let her know.

It was one of so many things he kept from her, though she knew he was trying to change that.

Being a bartender had honed her timing. She returned during the perfect lull in their conversation, setting the soft drink in front of Toby, who got one every time he came. "You may have heard about the trouble around here," she said to him.

"Oh, yeah. There're some pretty crazy rumors floating around."

Toby wasn't the type to go for a bunch of half-truths or white lies. So she gave Jacob credit for not pulling any punches. "Well, some of them are probably true," he said.

"You lost most of your cotton crop?" Toby asked, eyeing him over the rim of his glass.

KC stepped in, wanting to add a human element to the issues. Luckily, Toby was familiar with her family. He came here to eat or hang out just about every time he was in town. "It's really bad, Toby. Zach was the one who sprayed what he thought was pesticide, so he feels really responsible. You know how he is about that kind of stuff." Her brother's history of military service had desensitized him in many ways, but he'd become a quiet crusader for people in need, as his offer to help Jacob find the saboteur had shown.

"Wow," Toby said, glancing back and forth between them. "How'd that happen?"

KC didn't think Jacob was ready to be that forthcoming yet. Sure enough, he gave a generic "We still don't know. The important question is, how do we fix it?"

Toby was already shaking his head. "I've promised most of my crop out already. We're halfway to harvesttime. I've got orders to fill."

KC noted Jacob's restless shifting on the bar stool but ignored it. Instead, she turned on the charm with a look of feminine pleading. "Come on, Toby. We're talking about the livelihood of an entire town here. Couldn't you try to hunt us down *something* to help?" Hell, she'd even lean against the bar again if she had to.

"How much we talking about?" Toby said with an exaggerated sigh.

Sucker!

At that point, the conversation dissolved into a bunch of logistics that had KC's eyes glazing over. She was a people person, not a numbers person. And in the end, Toby was frowning.

"Please, Toby," she begged. Man, did she need to bat some eyelashes? "Isn't there anything you can do?"

His good ol' boy smile made an appearance. "Let me make some calls. You know I love ya, doll, but this is a tall order."

"We realize that," Jacob said, standing up. "But KC says if anyone can make it happen, you can."

Toby glanced her way, eliciting a grin of her own. "Did you really? I knew you were sweet on me."

KC could tell Jacob did not like that at all. "Like a brother, maybe," he said.

Ooh, possessive male glowering. Interesting. She raised a brow. "You'll have to overlook him, Toby. He's too serious for his own good."

Toby laughed. "Honey, the looks he's been shooting your way told me the whole story. You could at least give him a chance."

"Oh, he's had a chance," she confirmed, going full tease. "Now he thinks he's big stuff."

Jacob stepped closer, the intense look in his eyes speeding up her heartbeat. "I don't hear you complaining," he said.

Toby sputtered. "Wow, I never thought I'd see the day somebody tamed this kitty. I'll definitely see what I can do for ya."

What? Ignoring her squeal of outrage, Jacob handed over a business card.

Toby was barely on his way before KC was putting out a glare of her own. "What was that?" she demanded.

"You said I needed to have more fun," he said, but she wasn't buying that innocent look for a second. "Besides, all that teasing got us some cotton, didn't it?"

"I'm pretty sure it will," she said, a small glow of pride lighting inside her. She'd done it. If they could get even half the amount of cotton Toby had mentioned, the mill wouldn't have to go through layoffs and the town would be more secure. She'd already been in touch with Christina and Avery about the hardship fund.

Boy, it felt good to know she was making a difference.

But Jake wasn't through with her yet. "Still, we need to have a talk about your methods." He glanced down at her chest, reminding her of her tight T-shirt and accidental overexposure.

"Really?" Men had astounding audacity.

"Yes, really," he said, his voice deepening in that telltale way. He was so easy to read when he was aroused.

This time she deliberately leaned on the counter. Like clockwork, his gaze slid down. She chuckled. "We'll talk when you can keep your eyes on my face, dear."

Fifteen

KC struggled through the door to her house lugging Carter's car carrier—occupied by a crying Carter—his diaper bag, her purse, a grocery sack and box of diapers. She could have made two trips, but walking that many more steps through the pouring rain just wasn't in her plan for the day.

"Jake?" she called.

His SUV was outside, but the house sounded empty. At least from what she could hear over the wail of her child.

Dropping everything else to land wherever it would, she crossed to the coffee table to set Carter down. Those tearful eyes begging her to get him out while she maneuvered the straps were both pitiful and amusing. Boy, could he get to her. You'd think her leaving him in his car carrier this long was the end of the world.

Lifting him up against her shoulder, she crossed to the kitchen. Empty. Then she walked down the hall to her bedroom. Also empty. It wasn't until she was about to turn away that she registered the room itself. The drawers she'd emptied out for Jacob to use hadn't been closed completely, leaving the dresser with a slightly snaggletoothed look.

Moving around the bed, she saw a couple of T-shirts on

the floor. The dress clothes Jacob had worn to work this morning were tossed haphazardly over the small chaise occupying one corner. She lay Carter down in the center of the bed. With a trembling hand, she slid one of the drawers open to find clothes shoved about, instead of the neat little rows Jacob usually maintained. It was the same in his pants drawer.

Returning to her son, KC held him close. To other people, clothes on the floor might be an everyday occurrence, but Jacob was as obsessive about his environment as he was his schedule. Her house had never been cleaner. Jacob picked up after himself, and her, and Carter as he went through his day. It was something she thought he actually did unconsciously. He was just that neat of a person.

For the clothes to be askew? He'd been upset about something.

Back in the living room, she snatched up her purse as best she could with Carter in her arms and dug out her cell phone. Her heart skipped a beat when she saw a missed call, but it was just a girlfriend. A few swipes and she'd dialed Jacob. While she waited for him to answer, she jiggled Carter, who was starting to snuffle against her shirt—his precursor to demanding food.

Voice mail. *Dang it.* Should she leave a message? Call again? Carter started to wiggle, so she simply hung up and set the phone down so she could pat his back. "Okay, buddy," she said. "Let's get you some dinner, then we can track down Daddy."

Only, the longer she waited, the more time she had to think. About what could be wrong. About why he hadn't called. About where he was right now.

She and Carter had been settled in the chair with a bottle for about ten minutes when the doorbell rang. The baby startled, his eyes glancing toward the door, before returning to his dinner.

Jacob?

Of course not. Jacob had a key. Juggling the baby and bottle, KC went to the door and answered it. "Christina, thank goodness."

Christina might at least have some answers. Except Christina's tear-streaked face didn't do KC's sense of panic any good.

"Where's Jacob? What's wrong?"

"He and Aiden left midafternoon to go to North Carolina," Christina said as she came through the door and dripped on the carpet. KC was alarmed to see her friend didn't even have a raincoat or umbrella. "It's Luke. He had a car accident during a practice round." She glanced around as if unsure where she was or how she'd gotten here, turning almost in a circle before plopping onto the couch and letting her head fall into her hands. "I haven't heard an update since they got to the medical center in Charlotte, but his crew chief says it's pretty bad."

"Why didn't Jacob call and tell me?" *I'm simply a phone call away. Is that too hard?*

Christina was already shaking her head. "I'm sorry, KC. He was in total twin mode. That's why I figured I should come over here and tell you in person."

Twin mode. Oddly enough, she knew just what Christina meant. Jacob and Luke talked at least every other evening on the phone—and that was just what she saw here at home. She suspected they talked during the day, too. Or his phone would ring and Jacob would say, "That's Lucas," without even looking at the screen.

He had a connection to his brother she couldn't understand but did recognize. Had he thought she wouldn't?

Did that connection mean there wasn't room for her? Leaving town without even a simple text screamed she wasn't important enough to be told. She was simply a convenience, an obligation that came with his son.

In that moment, she knew she didn't want to be. She ached to mean enough to him to warrant that phone call.

To be truly needed. To be worthy of him sticking around—for her, not just for Carter.

Silence settled in the room as KC finished feeding Carter his bottle. The force of the wind spraying the rain against the windows added to KC's uneasiness.

Christina didn't seem to mind the silence. She simply sat there, probably not wanting to be alone. KC couldn't blame her.

Then the phone rang. From the ringtone, KC realized it was Christina's.

"Aiden," Christina said, relief raising her voice.

KC watched her as she settled Carter in his bouncy seat so he could kick his legs and reach for the little toys attached to it now that his tummy was full and he was happy.

Christina nodded several times as Aiden spoke, then closed her eyes in what looked like a painful squeeze. "Oh, Aiden," she breathed.

KC's heart pounded. *Please, let Luke be okay.*

Christina turned teary eyes in her direction and nodded. "Yes, I'm at her place now. Okay," she said, leaving KC frustrated with the one-sided conversation. If Aiden could talk to his wife, surely Jacob could call her, too.

Christina said her touching goodbyes to her husband and hung up without any word about KC. Obviously, Jacob hadn't asked for her.

"Aiden said the doctors are talking about more surgery tomorrow. He's gonna be okay eventually. But his legs are in pretty bad shape." Christina hugged herself and rocked a little. KC took a seat next to her and rubbed her back. Christina had always been friends with Luke. KC tried to remember that and how much her friend needed someone to comfort her with her husband a couple hundred miles away.

Not how that loathsome feeling of abandonment was once again spreading through her own mind and heart.

"But he's out of danger now?" KC asked quietly.

Christina nodded, a tear slipping down her cheek. Then

Carter blew a raspberry and the women laughed, breaking the tension.

"Come on," KC said as she stood. "Let's fix some dinner."

They were halfway through eating before KC trusted herself to ask without sounding needy, "Are they all okay?"

"They made it across the state line just before the storm hit, which worried me, since they were driving Aiden's car," Christina said. Then her eyes met KC's and the realization of what KC was asking dawned. "The doctors let Jacob stay in recovery with Lucas, but Aiden said he's hanging in there."

But Jacob couldn't step outside to update her personally? Even for a few minutes?

No. She wouldn't think like that. She simply nodded and moved on.

Not long after dinner, the local television station broke off programming for the announcement of Luke's accident.

KC wanted to ignore it, but she couldn't look away. Aiden and Jacob stood together behind a podium, forming a united front in stylish suits. But Jacob did the talking.

Across the bottom of the screen scrolled the words Local Celebrity Car Racer Severely Injured in Practice Accident. KC shivered as Jacob greeted the crowds of reporters. In their small-town life, it was easy to forget that all the Blackstone brothers had made names for themselves away from here.

"Good evening. I'm Jacob Blackstone." His calm, cultured voice washed over her, ramping up her need to be with him. *Beside him.* "Thank you for joining us today. Our family is deeply grateful for your concern over our brother, Luke 'Renegade' Blackstone."

She caught a barely perceptible shift from one foot to the other as Jacob paused. His face, usually a calm mask, had added stress lines across his forehead and a tightness around his mouth she wished she could ease with a gentle kiss.

He looked so tired, so worried, that guilt crept over her. Here he was in a life-or-death situation with his brother, and she was thinking only of herself. Still, that desire to comfort him wouldn't go away.

"Luke has suffered extensive damage to his legs," Jacob was saying, "along with broken ribs and other injuries. They are not life threatening, but we suspect he will be in recovery for a while."

Christina gasped, even though they'd already heard the news. Tears overflowed onto her pale cheeks.

"We ask that you bear with us as we learn more about Luke's medical needs and recovery. We will release more information as it becomes available. I'm sure, as much as he loves the spotlight, Luke will be happy to talk to y'all as soon as he's able."

A light round of laughter swept across the audience.

"Please respect our family's desire for privacy as we adjust. Thank you."

The men didn't stay for questions. Instead, they moved to a side door, where they exited with Luke's crew chief. The door closed behind them, leaving the reporters clamoring for more answers. KC felt left out in the cold, too.

After long moments of silence, Christina rose to her feet. "Are you sure you don't want to come stay at the manor with me?" she asked.

As much as KC wanted to comfort Christina, tonight's emotional roller coaster and the realization of her true feelings just as Jacob proved how shallow his were, meant she needed time alone. "I'm sorry, but it'll be easier to get Carter to sleep here. And I don't want to cart all his stuff over in the rain."

Christina's lips parted as if to speak, then her gaze slid away. "No problem. I completely understand."

KC really hoped so. She didn't want Christina to feel

as if she was abandoning her. "I'll call in the morning and check in, okay?"

But as Christina pulled out of the driveway, anger sparked in KC's heart. She could reach out, do the sympathetic, caring thing for her friend. But she couldn't do the same for Jacob because he'd cut off her access to him. And he refused to offer her the same consideration.

Yeah, she wouldn't be offering any sappy declarations of "luv" anytime soon. If ever… Instead, she piled in the chair, cuddling Carter in her arms. This was where she belonged…where she was loved. This was where she should stay.

Shouldn't she?

Jacob's back ached from his hours-long slump in the chair in the corner of his brother's hospital room. He'd heard nothing but the beep of the heart monitor and his own breathing for what seemed like forever. His gaze was trained in his brother's direction, but he was so tired he wasn't really seeing anything anymore. Still, he couldn't leave.

Since they were kids, Luke had been the reckless one, the one to take all the chances. It usually got him in trouble, but Jacob was always there to pick up the pieces. That was his role. He took care of his brother.

Even if all he could do was sit by his side in the hospital.

"What are you thinking?"

A minute or more passed before Jacob realized the voice was real and not a figment of his imagination. It was the husky, battered quality that convinced him his brother had actually spoken for the first time since his accident. Jerking to his feet, he crossed the space between them in seconds. "You're awake."

"What were you thinking?" Luke repeated.

Words Luke probably couldn't afford to waste, considering his current physical state.

Jacob grimaced. His thoughts had centered around only two things since they'd gotten into this room: Luke and KC. How Jacob wished she were here. Making him smile. Soothing him with her touch so his brain wouldn't run away with scenarios of his brother never walking again. But he couldn't say any of that to Luke. So he kept it bottled up and ached for her in silence.

"Just wondering whether you'd ever stop sleepin' the day away," he said instead.

Luke's half smile released the tension deep in Jacob's gut. "We can't all be boring, clock-watching suits like you."

It was an old argument between them. But there was a new undertone, slightly hazy from the painkillers.

Suddenly Aiden spoke from the doorway. "Good to finally see those peepers, brother."

As he walked toward the bed, Jacob noted that Aiden's spiky hair now spiked in a few different directions. He'd probably run his hands through his hair dozens of times last night. They'd both been worried, even after they moved Luke out of ICU.

"I just got off the phone with Christina," Aiden said. "Everyone at the manor is good. Not much damage from the storm. And I just saw your doctor down the hall, so she should be in soon."

Jacob's heart sped up. "Was KC with her?" He'd told Aiden to have Christina invite her to the manor. He worried about her and Carter being alone in her older house with a thunderstorm raging outside.

Aiden shook his head. "No, she didn't go home with Christina last night." He hesitated a moment, raising Jacob's suspicions.

"What?" he demanded.

"Christina says KC was pretty upset when she went over there. You really should have called her." Aiden looked down at Jacob's hand, then cocked his head in inquiry.

Jacob knew what was there: the cell phone he'd had in

his hand for hours. He'd picked it up with the intention of calling home, then thought about what he wanted to say, needed to say, and couldn't make himself dial the number.

He'd meant to call her sooner, but at first there'd been no thought for anything but Luke. This twin thing didn't come out often, but when it did, it was no joke. The feelings of responsibility that came with it were all consuming. Only later did Jacob let the outer world break through…

By then, his heart had been running scared. Acknowledging the words he'd said to her in the bar had been tough enough, though they hadn't discussed it. But Jacob knew they were true. He did love her. With an intensity as deep as his love for his brothers.

Now he stood in the hospital room of the brother he'd almost lost. His entire world had spiraled out of his control with the news that Luke had been in an accident. It had been like his father's death all over again.

Jacob wanted—no, needed—his control. Tight and locked down. But if he called KC, he'd be begging her to come to him, aching for her comfort and ultimately giving his control over to someone outside of himself.

"I'll talk to her, explain," he said, though he had no clue what he'd say.

"Dude." Luke's weak voice barely topped the monitors, but he kept going. "You'd better grovel."

Jacob knew his brother was right, but he couldn't act in the face of his fear. His fear and selfish actions had landed him in deep trouble.

Luke's doctor walked into the room, taking Jacob's mind off the looming disaster back home. She moved directly to the bed, zeroing in on her patient. After a quick examination and a few questions, she addressed the elephant in the room. "Luke, I'm not going to lie to you, this is going to be a long recovery," she said.

Luke blinked slowly at the doctor, as if he couldn't quite take in what was being said.

"You will recover. Eventually. But with compound fractures this bad, in both legs, you'll need time to heal, then lots of work to rebuild your muscle strength and ability to walk. And that's not even addressing your other injuries."

Jacob looked at his brother, his leanly muscled body so still for once, and knew exactly what was going through his mind. Luke wouldn't care about pain, or rebuilding his strength—he'd only care about one thing. "His racing?" Jacob asked, feeling his throat close around the words.

She shook her head. "I don't know. The physical requirements of the sport might end up being too much, especially on his feet. It all depends on how he heals." She grinned at the prone man. "Which means you have to *take orders* and do the work."

"Oh, I'm used to work," Luke teased, though his smile was a mere stretch of tight lips. Jacob could feel the ache of Luke's sadness echo inside his own chest. "But I'm not takin' orders from nobody."

And wasn't that the truth? His brother could be as stubborn as they come—he was a Blackstone after all.

But the doctor smiled, probably as happy as Jacob to see Luke even attempt a joke at this devastating setback. "I guess that's the best I can hope for. We're gonna keep you here for now. See if there needs to be one more surgery, and make sure no infection sets into the places where the bone broke through your skin."

Jacob winced inwardly but maintained as much outward calm as he could manage. Normally, that was easy. Today, not so much.

"I'll let y'all know how things look tomorrow and give you a better time line for what's gonna happen. Just rest and let the antibiotics do their job."

Luke nodded, his eyes already drifting closed again.

Jacob and Aiden followed the doctor to the door, where she paused to look back at her patient. "Jacob, your twin is going to need you a lot, especially over the next few months. I understand that you live in South Carolina?"

"Yes," Jacob confirmed. "Down on the coastal side. Farther away than I'd like."

"I would consider finding him rehab options closer to home. I think he'll weather the upcoming difficulties much better surrounded by his family. Let me look into what's available in your area."

"Thank you, Doctor," Aiden said, then escorted her out into the hall. Leaving Jacob once more alone with Luke.

He pulled his cell phone out of his pocket once more, staring at the screen for long moments. He felt shaky, off guard. The past six months had been one change after another. Moving home. His job. Carter. This new, different relationship with KC.

He knew he needed her to steady his world and keep him strong. But he was supposed to be the strong one. He wasn't supposed to lean on someone else. And that was exactly what he wanted to do.

His hands started to shake, forcing him to tighten them into fists. His cell phone case dug into the edges of his palm.

So this was why he'd kept his relationship with KC simple and below the radar. Giving up his heart meant giving up control. Hell, he wasn't even sure he was capable of doing that.

He'd lost his dad. He'd almost lost Luke. Was he seriously considering adding another ticking time bomb to his life?

I love you. Immediately his mind recalled the warmth of KC's body cuddled against his in the dead of night. The spike of joy in his chest the first time Carter had smiled at him. The ache of need that grew with every minute he was away from them both.

Well, damn. It looked as if it was a little too late to fight this one off. "Wow," he heard from the bed. "That's some pretty intense stuff going on in that brain of yours. If you need someone to talk to, I can listen."

Jacob glanced over to find Luke's eyes open once more. "I know." Luke might offer to listen, but he had enough on his plate at the moment.

"I have nothing better to do. And I'll be asleep half the time anyway, so there's no need to be embarrassed. Just get it off your chest, dude."

Why not? His brother's drug-induced haziness made things a little easier to say. Maybe after, Luke wouldn't remember Jacob being so weak. "I screwed up, leaving her like that."

"You sure did."

All he'd been able to think about was getting to Luke. His logical brain had reasoned that KC couldn't travel on such short notice because of Carter, but it had all been excuses.

"I'm such an idiot," he said. How could he have convinced himself it would be better for KC to hear the news about Luke from anyone but him? He'd been worried about maintaining his gold-star control by keeping her at arm's length, worried he might toss aside his pride and beg her to come to him. Had he once thought about how all of this affected her?

"I've told you that a lot but you never listen," Luke said in an almost singsong voice, suggesting to Jacob that another dose of pain meds must have been delivered through the IV.

"I know, brother," Jacob murmured as Luke's eyes drifted closed. "This time, ignoring you isn't gonna work."

"Call her," Luke murmured. Then his eyes were shut tight, and that intangible connection between them broke.

Heart pounding, though he'd never admit it, Jacob slipped out the door and found Aiden in the hall. "Could you sit with Luke for a few minutes?"

Aiden's brows jumped toward his hairline. "Why would you even have to ask?"

Because taking care of Luke was *his* responsibility. "Right." He cleared his throat. "Can I use your phone?"

"Why?" Aiden asked with a frown.

"My battery is dead."

"Of course," Aiden said, handing it over. Jacob ignored Aiden's knowing look and headed for the stairs with the phone. Two minutes later, he was outside, staring across the dark alleyway behind the hospital as he listened to the ring on the other end of the line. He couldn't go out front—there were too many reporters hanging around. The staff had said this little area was secure if they needed to smoke or anything.

"Hello?"

KC's tentative voice caused emotion to tighten his throat, forcing him to clear it. "KC?" Then he remembered he wasn't on his own phone. "It's me. Jacob."

For a minute, he thought she wouldn't answer. When her soft "Hey" came across the line, sweet relief ran through his veins. Maybe just a moment too soon, because that was all she said.

Struggling to fill the silence, Jacob relayed the doctor's findings. But when he paused to draw a breath, KC broke in, "I know. I saw you on television."

"Right." Had she been all alone? Or had Christina still been there? "The press have been crazy here. Camped out all over the hospital grounds, trying to get in the doors… One even sneaked in through the emergency room then tried to grill a nurse for information on Luke." He grinned at the memory of their night nurse telling an animated version of the story. "Luke might start to think he's hot stuff."

"I bet he will." She spoke the words, but there was no life in them. He was definitely in the doghouse.

Not only was she quiet, but it sounded as if the house

was, too. His voice softened at the thought of his son. "Carter asleep?"

"Yes."

"Did the storm keep him up last night?"

"Some."

What about you? he wanted to ask. *Did it keep you awake? Did you wish I was there? Because I wish you were here.* Did he have the courage to say it? "The house okay?"

"Yes. It's stood for fifty years. It'll stand for fifty more."

This awkward conversation was not going the way he wanted, but he had no one but himself to blame.

"Listen, Jacob, I need to go to bed. It's been a long day, and like I said, we didn't sleep very well last night."

"Neither did I." He drew in a deep breath. *Time to suck it up, big man.* "Without you."

"I'm sure," she murmured.

"KC?"

"Yes?"

I'm sorry I'm such an idiot? No. Probably the wrong approach. "I love you, and wish you could be here with me."

She didn't ask the obvious: *So why didn't you give me the chance?* Instead, she whispered, "Thank you," and hung up the phone.

Sixteen

Aiden stepped into the room the next day right after the lunch lady cleaned up Luke's tray. If one could call broth "lunch." "You have a visitor," he said.

"I don't think he's up to it yet," Jacob said, noting Luke's groggy stare trained on his brother.

"Not him, dummy. You," Aiden said.

Who could possibly be here to see him?

"She was just gonna drop off your stuff and go," Aiden said, "but I told her to wait."

Stuff. KC was here? Jacob was through the door in the fastest move he'd executed since his mad dash to reach Luke. Stepping into the hall was easier this time than all the times before because his connection with his brother no longer pulled like a taut rubber band between them. As Luke's pain diminished, the wound on the twin brothers' psyches was beginning to heal, as well. For Jacob, it was now a barely noticeable twinge.

It would be a much longer road for Luke.

A few steps brought her into view. He'd expected a display of anger or even rejection. Instead, her face was an impassive mask, not really telling him anything.

He didn't know where to start, except with the obvious. "What're you doing here?"

A flash of uncertainty broke through the mask for a single second, but just as quickly disappeared. "I know you left in a hurry," she said, the words rushing from those perfectly shaped lips. "Too quickly to get your stuff. So I brought your travel bag." She gestured to his black bag on the floor next to her feet. "Some clothes, those protein bars you like for breakfast..."

Wow, fresh clothes. Jacob's outfit was rumpled, and he reeked after sleeping in a chair for three days. He'd already rotated through the two outfits he'd grabbed to bring with him. He simply didn't have it in him to leave the hospital, much less go to a store for something.

Her hard swallow drew his gaze to her throat. This seemed as difficult for her to say as it was for him to listen. "When you're ready to leave the hospital, Aiden will have a suitcase for you at his hotel room. Including your laptop. He put it in his car for you."

Holy smokes. She'd thought of everything. But then again, this was KC. Had he thought she'd do anything less?

"And I thought you might eventually need this." She pulled a gray cord out of her pocket—his phone charger. "You left it beside the bed."

"KC, thank you. This...this is very thoughtful. Did you drive up?" Man, that would have been hard for her. Crack of dawn was not something KC did well.

She shook her head. "No, Zachary flew me up. Just a quick trip."

"You flew?" His mind automatically went back to the day they'd met...and just how scared she was of flying. Which made her presence now even more incredible. "I don't know what to say." Especially since he'd left her behind without a word. Literally.

The difficulty of having this conversation and speaking to her after what he'd said on the phone...

Jacob hated this. They were so stiff with each other—avoiding eye contact, talking but not really saying anything. All his fault. All of it.

"There's nothing to say," she said, though her gaze was a bit too solemn for his liking. "We're partners. I just want to help any way I can." She gestured to the bag. "This I knew I could do."

What impressed him wasn't her words, but her tone. She could have called him out for ignoring her, for leaving town without notifying her or even for not calling personally for over twenty-four hours. But she didn't.

He could do no less. "I'm sorry, KC. I didn't have time to prepare."

"And we all know you like to be prepared, Jake," she said with a smirk, but her gaze still wouldn't lift to his.

That was probably why all this had thrown him for a loop in the first place. The plan was all-important to him. Now he needed to set that aside and he wasn't even sure how.

"KC, I know this is going to sound cowardly, but when I get home, can we talk?" This time those beautiful hazel eyes peeked from beneath her lashes. As their gazes met, he could see the same awareness that he'd heard permeating every word between them on their phone call. "There are some things, more things I need to say, starting with I'm sorry. But you deserve better than a rushed apology in a hospital hallway."

To his surprise, a sheen of tears graced her eyes. "I'd like that," she murmured.

"Thank you," he said simply, and then tried to get the conversation off more emotional topics before he pulled her close and refused to let her go. "Your mom got a handle on things with Carter?"

She swiped her fingers across each eye before nodding. "Yes, but that reminds me." Reaching into her own oversize tote bag, she pulled out a white paper sack. "She sent these because she said none of you should be forced to live on hospital food." She held it out like a white truce flag.

Jacob opened it, only to be seduced by the sweet aroma of a couple dozen peanut-butter cookies. "Wow," he said, not wasting any time shoving a whole one in his mouth. As the creamy, crunchy treat dissolved on his tongue, he couldn't hold back a moan.

"I'll take that to mean the cookies are appreciated," she said with a wistful smile. "I'll be sure to let Mom know."

"I must be weakening her barriers against me." This time, he actually got KC to share his grin.

"Jacob, the doctor is here," Aiden called from across the hall.

Jacob nodded before turning back to KC. "I need to go." He'd tried to be present for every update, worried about these first few steps of healing. But now he was pulled in the opposite direction.

He wanted her with him, even if it was only for a little longer. "Could you… Would you come with me?"

The surprise on her face reminded him of all he'd kept to himself. Everything she'd never been a part of. He'd claimed it was to keep her and Carter safe, but was it really? Had he been protecting her or himself?

He'd demanded they behave like a family—24/7—yet he'd failed to mingle the two most important halves of his life.

Gently taking her hand in his, he led her across the hallway and into Luke's room. The doctor was already speaking with Aiden and Luke about the additional surgery he'd be having the next morning. Resignation strained Luke's already pale features. He remained silent while his brothers asked all the pertinent questions.

Luke's sadness crept over Jacob, and he squeezed KC's hand tight. He simply couldn't let go. Even when the doctor extended her hand before she left, Jacob moved KC's hand into his other one so he could shake.

"Doctor, this is KC Gatlin."

After a quick glance at their joined hands, the doctor gave him an understanding look. "Don't worry," she told them both. "He will get through this."

Whether she meant Luke or himself, Jacob wasn't completely sure.

As she left, he felt KC's thumb rub along his. The fact that she would offer him comfort humbled him. After all he'd done, she still stood here with him. He led her forward to Luke's bedside.

Luke adopted a semblance of his trademark grin. "Wow, is this what I have to do to get pretty visitors?"

Jacob groaned. "Stop flirting with my woman, you egomaniac."

KC grinned, bumping her side against Jacob's. "Don't give your brother a hard time." She reached out to brush her free hand over Luke's. "I'm very sorry, Luke. If there's anything I can do for you…"

"Oh, just make sure I get to meet that cute little nephew of mine when I come back into town." His grin was a short-lived flash of brilliance. "Gives me something to look forward to."

Jacob heard her quick catch of breath, but no tears this time. "I sure will," she said. "But for now, I'll let you rest. I really need to get back to the airport. My brother is waiting to take me home."

Jacob was once again reminded of how scared to death she must have been in that little bitty plane, but she'd still flown all the way here—just to bring him what she thought he would need. KC was a giving person, but this was something more.

And he had to make sure he was worthy of it.

"I'll be back after I get her safely on her way," Jacob said. Aiden acknowledged him with an understanding nod, and then Jacob led KC out the door.

There were complications to visiting here. Paparazzi

were everywhere. If she was seen arriving or leaving the hospital with him, word would spread quickly. The vultures would hunt down her story in seconds, and he refused to leave her unprotected.

One of the nurses called a cab for them. Jacob walked KC down to a back corridor where security guarded an outside entrance. This way he could ensure her safe departure without interference from unwanted visitors. After only a few short minutes of waiting, Jacob gave into his need and wrapped his arms around her. He guided her head to rest against his chest, stroking his hand along her silky hair in an effort to soothe her.

Looking down at her guarded face, he knew she was still worried he'd walk away—indeed, he had without a word. But she made no demands. Gave no ultimatums. "I just don't know what to say. You could have really dug into me for behaving like an—" He stopped when she shook her head.

"I was angry. I've had too many men walk away in my life not to be."

The reminder of her childhood made him feel even lower.

"But then I realized something. The question isn't whether or not you go without me, Jacob. Life happens. I understand that. What really matters is whether or not I'm part of the decision. Part of the plan. That's what's important. And totally up to you. I will not be an obligation to you, Jacob. This is something you have to decide for yourself."

She was trusting him. He refused to disappoint her.

"Jacob, now," Aiden said as he slipped back into Luke's room.

"I'll call," Jacob murmured against her hair.

All too soon the cab arrived. She gave him a quick kiss, then started to walk away. She seemed completely unaware he was shaking inside from her gesture.

Her actions drove home exactly how deep he was in this relationship, because he wanted to meet her expectations, not just his obligations toward their son.

With just a few quick strides he was once again by her side. He cupped her face between his hands, guiding it up so he could brush his lips over hers. Once for the hello he'd failed to give. Once for the goodbye he hated to say. And once more as a promise. "I'll be home soon."

As he headed back into his brother's room, Jacob made a decision. As soon as he was sure Luke was stable, it was time to go home to his new family and win KC back.

In the way she truly deserved.

Jacob stood outside the door to Lola's, listening to the sounds of a busy Friday night. The parking lot was packed with cars. It should have been like any other Friday when he left work and had dinner with Aiden in the corner booth, watching his woman from across the room as she worked the bar.

Not tonight, he thought with a leap in his stomach. Tonight, he would finally make it official.

He'd stayed in Charlotte another few days after KC's surprise visit, long enough to make sure that Luke was well on his way to recovery. It would take time, but his brother would get back on his feet.

But he was sidelined from racing for the foreseeable future. Jacob didn't want to consider the emotional implications of that prognosis. Luke took every lick with a smile and a laugh, much the way he had when they were kids. But Jacob could see the shadows behind the laughter. His heart ached for his brother. But Jacob had come to a point of desperation: he had to get home to KC and Carter. Sure, they'd talked a few times on the phone after she'd left Charlotte—mostly about the baby. And KC never asked when Jacob was coming home or complained about him not being there.

Most men would be thrilled, but not Jacob. He hated that she didn't feel worthy of placing those demands on him. But with her family history, he understood why she didn't. It was up to him to show her those demands were her right. That she shouldn't let men take advantage of her—even him.

But the things Jake wanted to say, well, they shouldn't be said over the phone.

Jacob had finally acknowledged that he needed KC with him. But when Luke moved home soon, Jacob had to be with him, too. Once Luke's doctor released him, they were going to move him back to Blackstone Manor and do his physical therapy here. Luke was gonna need help, which meant things had to change. Jacob couldn't be in two places at once, and there was no room at KC's place for his brother. Jacob had a choice to make. His brother was an obligation he couldn't—no, wouldn't—turn his back on. But leaving KC and Carter alone put them in danger, and wasn't even an option anyway. The past few days had shown him he didn't want to be just a part-time dad…or a part-time lover.

So he'd made his choice. Would KC make the same one?

"You gonna go through that door or just stare at it all night?"

Jacob threw a dirty look at Zachary over his shoulder. As usual, it didn't faze KC's brother.

"Sis know you're back in town?"

Jacob turned back to the door. "No. I just got here."

"Okay," Zachary drew the word out. "So seriously. Why are you hovering outside the door like a mother hen?"

"I'm not, you goof. I'm just trying to decide what to say…"

"Yeah, laying your heart bare can be a little difficult. I'd hesitate, too."

Jacob threw a sidelong glance at the other man. He was awfully chipper for a guy the police still considered a prime suspect in a major felony case. “She said she trusted me to come back to her.”

“Finally figured it out, didn’t ya?”

“You know, I’ve had money all my life, but her trust in me? That’s one of the most precious gifts I’ve ever been given.”

Zachary nodded.

“I’d better be damn sure not to break it,” Jacob concluded.

“Bingo. I think you’ve got this figured out.” Zachary spread his hands wide. “My work here is done.” Then he looked Jacob straight in the eye. “Did you hear? KC’s been doing a great job getting the charity started. And Toby secured us some cotton, thanks to KCs skills as a negotiator. We’re good to go for fall.”

“Thank goodness. I knew putting her in charge was the right move.”

“Trust me, putting Sis in charge is always the right move.” As Zachary walked away, he said over his shoulder, “Hope you made sure the ring was spectacular.”

Damn, that man was a mind reader. Jacob did have a ring, but that wasn’t the most important thing he was offering tonight.

Determined now, he marched through the door and made his way straight to the bar, not looking left or right. Only KC, dead ahead in his sights, mattered. His heart tried to crawl up his throat before he reached her.

Man, was she beautiful. He watched as she pulled a beer with naturally confident moves, smiling at the customer with graciousness and a hint of flirtation. He wanted to growl out that she was his, but she wasn’t—not so long as he chose to keep her a secret, as if she wasn’t important enough to be an acknowledged part of his life.

That was about to change.

She saw him and smiled her casual smile, sticking to

the routine of the past months. Only the slight widening of her eyes gave away her surprise.

"We need to talk," he said, nodding toward an unoccupied corner of the bar.

He could tell from her slow steps that she wasn't sure she wanted to follow him. But it seemed that she couldn't stop herself. "Jacob, you don't have to—" she said from behind him.

"Yes," he said, cutting her off. "You may not need the words, but I do. I need to explain what happened while I was away."

Her eyes widened. He'd given her no reason to expect this, no reason to anticipate him doing anything more than waltzing back home as if nothing had changed. But it had. He had.

He came around the bar into the forbidden bartender zone, not caring who was watching. "I'll be honest. I don't know if this is the right thing to say. I know it's not the most romantic or charming. It wasn't until I got to the hospital that I realized, if I called you, the only thing I'd ask was for you to come. To be there with me."

She shook her head. "Why didn't you? Why didn't you ask me to stay?"

"Uprooting you, disrupting Carter's schedule… It made no logical sense."

"But I would do it because I love you. That's what people do. Not shove the people who love them away because they aren't convenient for them."

"You're right. You aren't convenient."

Her wince told him that stung a little. But his point wasn't a soft one.

"Neither is how I feel about you. Or Carter. I want everything to fit in its little compartment and you don't… Which is a good thing."

"I *really* don't understand."

Her welling eyes made him feel like such a jackass.

"I'm rigid in my own ways, sort of like my grandfather. I like consistency. Logic. Rules. You are none of those things. And I want you more than anything." Shaking his head, he couldn't hold back an unexpected grin.

"I left. I didn't call. I had reasons—my battery died, I couldn't leave Luke's bedside, there were paparazzi everywhere and things to take care of. But I figured out they were just excuses…and not even good ones."

He moved in closer, anxious to feel her body heat against his. She threw a glance to the side, looking over the crowd, but for once he couldn't care less who was watching.

"I screwed up, KC. The truth is, I was afraid. If I had called you, I'd have dissolved into a blubbering mess begging you to join me."

Now he had her full attention. "But I still don't understand why that's a bad thing," she said, reaching up to rub the curve of his jaw.

"It's just a thing I'm not used to. Something I don't know how to handle." His laugh was dry. Half-angry. "Aiden, Luke and I—we've stood on our own since our father died. Not relying on anyone else. I don't know how to change that. But I have to try, because these feelings aren't going away."

He ducked his head to nuzzle her soft hand. "I know I won't handle things the way you want me to. Emotions and life and fear. But I will always come back to you and Carter. Always. Not because I have to, because I want to."

Her expression was wide-eyed and wondrous. Was it happiness…or fear?

Or both?

As she took a tentative step toward him, the DJ took a break. Perfect timing.

The music faded from the room, leaving the sound of people making their way to the bar for another drink. But she had eyes only for him. Out of his peripheral vision, he saw her brother serving the patrons lining up at the bar. Then a mischievous grin spread across her lips.

"So what is it I can get you, Jacob Blackstone?"

Her sexy confidence, mixed with carefully cloaked need, melted every last ounce of resistance inside him. "You, KC Gatlin."

He spoke loud enough for the words to carry to those behind them. After that, the speed of gossip in a small town took over. By the time she asked, "What?" he had the attention of half the bar.

"KC, I only need one thing," he said with a small grin. He let his palms flatten on the smooth counter behind her to ground himself, ground them. "Would you and Carter come live with me at Blackstone Manor?"

She joined in the collective gasp, her big eyes even rounder now. She glanced at the crowd. "Jacob, what are you saying?"

"I'm saying my mother needs me at home. My brother will need me there very soon. But in the midst of all of that, I want to give you what *you* need. Please come with me. Don't make me go alone."

"But I don't belong—"

He stopped her protest with a kiss. "You're the best thing that could have happened to me. I'm just sorry it took me so long to do something about it."

The whispers rippled across the room. Heavy footsteps sounded behind him. "Come on, KC," Aiden said. "Put us all out of our misery and accept the poor guy. His moping is driving me crazy."

Jacob glanced over to Zachary. "Zachary, may I?" Jacob asked, garnering permission in more ways than one.

KC's brother gave a short nod and a smile. "Be my guest."

In seconds, Jacob had the ring in his hand.

"I thought you didn't like public displays," she said, examining the princess-cut emerald that matched the green that was flashing in her eyes.

He tilted her chin up with his finger to get a look at the real thing. “Sweetheart, with you, I’ll take you any way I can have you. And I’d rather the world know you were mine than risk for a moment the chance of being without you.”

“But what about…” She glanced around at their audience, then leaned closer and whispered, “The mill, the crazy person threatening people? You said it wasn’t safe.”

“I promise you now, I will not let him ever harm you or Carter, no matter what it takes.” He pulled her closer, now whispering in her ear, “KC, I love what we’ve built together. But I need you with me, in every part of my life. Will you marry me? Please?”

“Jacob, don’t you know I’d follow you anywhere? All you had to do was ask me.”

As the cheers erupted around them, he let his lips speak his gratitude against hers.

Seventeen

Later that night—long after all the excitement had died down, Jacob had bought a few rounds and Zachary had offered to close up for the night—KC finally had Jacob to herself. He opted for a long, hot shower to wash off his travel fatigue. When he came out of the bathroom, KC was in bed, staring at her new ring.

"Is Carter asleep?" he asked.

"Yes, I just got him back down." Her little man's excitement at seeing his daddy again had simply added to the night's joy.

Jacob reached for her hand, rubbing over her fingers right above the band. "I realized something while I was in the shower."

"What's that?"

"I didn't tell you the most important part."

Yep, KC's heart was definitely gonna explode.

"I told you I was too logical." He grinned in a self-deprecating way that warmed her, because Jake was usually the confident one. "I do love you, KC. You've changed me, you and Carter both. For the better, I hope."

I believe you. The words trembled on her lips. She wanted to say them so badly, but all she could think about was her daddy leaving for the store one day and never coming back. Logically, she knew it wasn't the same. But her woman's heart wouldn't give up the fear.

"KC, do you remember what I told your mother and grandmother?"

She looked over at him sitting on the corner of their bed. She felt like a kid who'd been given permission to go crazy in the candy store but was afraid the sugar might kill her. "When?"

"That first Sunday dinner? Your grandmother asked me how she could know that I was trustworthy."

Oh, right. She nodded, afraid to speak as his words brought a lifetime of thoughts rushing to the surface.

"I told her then and I'll tell you now—me promising to always be here, to put you and Carter first is all well and good. But they're just words. Instead, I'll have to prove it to you through my actions."

"Like taking our relationship public in a major way?"

"Oh, yes. But in my defense, your brother egged me on."

"What?"

He grinned, reaching out to hold her hand, turning it so that her engagement ring caught the light. "He's really sneaky, that one. But seriously, it will take time, and I may make mistakes, but I'll prove it to you and Carter. Every day."

Jacob was looking at her as if all her secrets were already known. As if he knew he couldn't force a response, he changed tactics. "Would you come to bed with me?"

Oh, boy. She should be more than ready to jump into bed with the man who'd just asked her to marry him. But her emotions were all over the place, her thoughts racing… "I don't know." Why did she feel as if she was being put through an endurance test?

"Not for sex," Jacob said, surprising her. His sincerity shone from his amber eyes. "Right now, I need something more."

More? She'd always thought men saw sex as the ultimate expression of their emotions. And in a way, it would be easier to go back to that sexual focus. But she needed more—and she wanted to give Jacob the opportunity to prove himself to her in a way no man had bothered to do before now.

"I love you, KC, and after everything that's happened between us, I can't think of anything better than to spend a few hours just lying in your arms." His voice deepened, his face twisting with emotion. "I need you."

Minutes later, as she sank against him in their bed, no longer alone and abandoned, she knew she could let go of the fear. "I love you, too," she whispered.

Less than a week later, KC took the one step she'd resisted since Jake's return to her life. Fear and excitement settled in a tingly mass in the pit of her stomach as she stood before the elaborately carved entrance to Blackstone Manor. Even the lion door knocker intimidated her, which was saying a lot. Usually she was pretty hard to rattle.

Standing confidently by her side, Jacob said, "Welcome home."

She clung to the happiness in Jake's eyes as if it was her own personal life preserver. She wasn't used to this kind of wealth; most of her life, she'd had an average amount of money, though she had vague memories of some financial struggles after her dad hit the road.

But a house this size, the luxurious grounds, someone to cook, to clean… She was totally out of her element.

Even Christina's welcoming smile didn't calm KC's nerves about fitting in. Holding a sleeping Carter in her arms like a shield, she let Jacob escort her inside, despite a deep-rooted desire to return to her little house on the other end of town.

But it wasn't long before the residents were welcoming her as if she were a long-lost daughter. Nolen smiled as he greeted her. The look in his faded blue eyes was sincere as he encouraged her to let him know if she needed a hand with anything. Marie didn't have any of the older man's reserve. She embraced KC and Carter together, then oohed and aahed over the baby.

Jacob grinned. "Now, I don't wanna start a rivalry, so I won't comment on your mom's peanut-butter cookies in front of Marie..."

The cook frowned in his direction.

"But Marie's chocolate-chip cookies are the best I've ever tasted. If you smell them baking, better get to the kitchen. They go fast."

Leaving the beaming cook behind, Jacob showed KC where everything was on the first floor. With a mysterious intensity, he said, "Do you want to see our suite?"

She looked up the elegant, sweeping staircase to the second floor. "Actually, don't you think it's time I met your mother?"

His gaze sobering, Jacob led her up the staircase and to the right. KC paused and nodded toward the opposite side of the hall. An open set of double doors revealed a room under construction. "What's that?"

"That used to be my grandfather's suite." He squeezed her shoulder. "We're renovating it for Luke because it's closest to the elevator."

She met his look, seeing all the worry and exhaustion over his brother's injuries, emotions Jake kept well hidden—except in the darkest hours of the night when he held her close.

Then Jacob led them into a feminine suite decorated in shades of lavender. Lily Blackstone lay as still as a frozen angel, her only movement the lift of her chest as she breathed.

As they approached the bed, Jacob said, "KC, this is my mom, Lily."

His hushed voice held respect and tenderness. KC

watched the comatose woman in silence for long moments, thinking about her own mother and her love for Carter. With a small smile, she left the warmth of Jacob's arms and crossed to the side of the bed opposite all the medical equipment. "Ms. Blackstone," she said. "This is your grandson, Carter."

Then she slipped her son into the gap between Lily's arm and her side, cradling his head against his grandmother's warm body.

Carter continued to sleep soundly as KC talked. "He looks a lot like Jacob and Luke. Jacob says they both had these same blond curls when they were babies. He has Jake's feet, too—long and a little narrow—"

After a few more minutes by Lily's side, KC felt Jacob's presence behind her. Though she twisted his way, he didn't give her the chance to glimpse his face. Instead, he buried his head into the crook of her shoulder, his arms drawing her close.

He stood like that for a long time—silent, shaking—until he finally pulled back. It was reminiscent of the night he'd asked her to marry him, long after they'd lain down in bed together. Finally looking down, his amber eyes were dry but glowing with emotion.

"Thank you." Two simple words—it was amazing how much they meant to her.

Then he kissed his mother's cheek and scooped Carter back into his arms. Their son's eyes peeked open for a minute, then closed once more after he'd reassured himself that Daddy was there.

"I've got something to show you," Jacob said, taking her hand to lead her back down the hallway and up two more flights of stairs.

"I can see I've got my work cut out for me," she teased, huffing a little at the climb.

Jacob paused. "I should have taken you to the elevator."

"Are you kidding? My legs are gonna look great after a month of this."

He grinned, stepping close to brush his lips across hers. "No, KC, it's hard to improve on perfection."

She loved that he would let himself tease and be teased now. "Flattery will get you everywhere, Mr. Blackstone... So will hefting the baby up these stairs for me."

They continued to the third floor, this time turning left at the top of the stairs. "We'll be close to the elevator, too. I'm just used to taking the stairs unless I have my hands full," Jacob said, adjusting Carter in his arms.

She ran an appreciative eye over the main room, decorated in various shades of green. Then Jacob led her through a door on the other side. "We have a good chunk of this floor," he said as he led her through what looked like a walk-in closet. "There's a single bedroom on the other side that Aiden uses for storage, since the room he shares with Christina isn't very big. And another empty room."

"And what else?" KC asked, mentally adding up all the square footage on the floor and marveling at the size of the place.

"This."

Jacob opened the door onto a baby boy's wonderland nursery. Walls painted a green shade to match the other room. A race-car theme, which made KC smile. Everything a baby and mama could need, including a snuggle chair built similarly to the one in her living room. "Wow, Jacob. This is beautiful. Did Christina do this for you?"

He raised his brows in mock offense. "Heck, no. I did this myself. Even assembled the crib."

He'd done it all himself... Jacob had been gone for a while, and there hadn't been enough time for him to do it since his return. So that meant... "You started this as soon as you knew," she breathed.

"I did, KC." He moved over to the crib and settled Carter inside. When he turned back, his gorgeous eyes were clouded over, bringing out their brown highlights. "I want you to know I didn't do this to show off or outdo you. I guess…I hoped you'd see that I was invested—in him, in us, something other than work."

"I'm glad," she said, the beauty around her feeling right. It wasn't pretentious, didn't have the cold look of someone trying to show off. But each color, each item spoke of love for a baby and his comfort. "It's perfect."

Sliding into his arms felt just as right.

"I love you, KC. I'll never leave either of you again. You can trust me."

"I'll never leave you, either," she said, and knew deep down how very true her words were. "Family sticks together, right?"

"Right." He granted her a beautiful smile. "That sounds like the perfect plan to me."

* * * * *

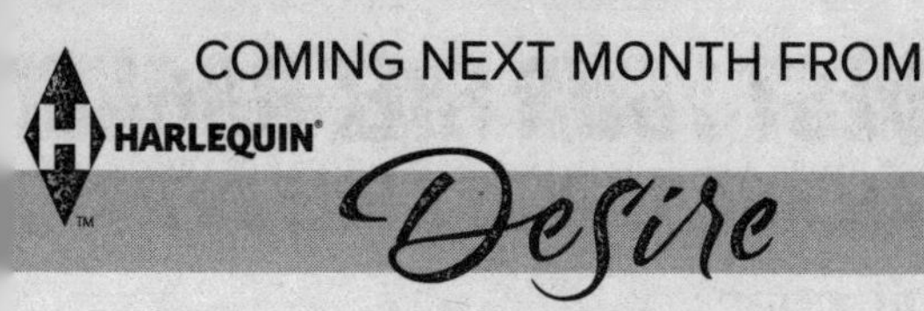

Available March 3, 2015

#2359 ROYAL HEIRS REQUIRED

Billionaires and Babies • by Cat Schield

Love and duty collide as Prince Gabriel Alessandro weds Lady Olivia Darcy to assume his nation's throne. But when he discovers he's the secret father of twin girls, will all bets be off?

#2360 MORE THAN A CONVENIENT BRIDE

Texas Cattleman's Club: After the Storm
by Michelle Celmer

What could be simpler than a marriage of convenience between friends? That's what star Texas surgeon Lucas Wakefield and researcher Julie Kingston think, until a jealous ex shows up and throws a wrench in their plans.

#2361 AT THE RANCHER'S REQUEST

Lone Star Legends • by Sara Orwig

It was a dark and stormy night when billionaire rancher Mike Calhoun rescued the stranded motorist. Now the widower has a storm in his own life as he's torn by unwanted attraction to this pregnant, vulnerable beauty...

#2362 AFTER HOURS WITH HER EX

by Maureen Child

When prodigal son Sam Wyatt comes home to his family's ski resort, he must work with his estranged wife to keep the business alive. But does this mean new life for the relationship he left behind?

#2363 PREGNANT BY THE SHEIKH

The Billionaires of Black Castle • by Olivia Gates

Numair can reclaim his birthright and gain the power of two thrones by marrying Jenan. And Jenan is more than willing to provide an heir for this delicious man—until she discovers his true agenda.

#2364 THE WEDDING BARGAIN

The Master Vintners • by Yvonne Lindsay

Shanal will sacrifice everything, even wed her unlovable boss, for her destitute parents' sakes. But when she gets cold feet at the altar, it's white knight Raif to the rescue. Will their desire be her redemption?

SPECIAL EXCERPT FROM

HARLEQUIN®

Desire

When Julie Kingston enters into a green-card marriage with her best friend and boss, she gets more than she bargained for...

Read on for a sneak preview of
USA TODAY *bestselling author*
Michelle Celmer's
MORE THAN A CONVENIENT BRIDE

*~ A **TEXAS CATTLEMAN'S CLUB: AFTER THE STORM** novel ~*

"We'll have to kiss," she heard Luc say, and it took her brain a second to catch up with her ears.

"Kiss?"

"During the wedding ceremony," he said.

"Oh, right." Julie hadn't considered that. She thought about kissing Luc, and a peculiar little shiver cascaded down the length of her spine. Back when she'd first met him, she used to think about the two of them doing a lot more than just kissing, but he had been too hung up on Amelia and their recently broken engagement to even think about another woman. So hung up that he'd left his life in Royal behind and traveled halfway around the world with Doctors Without Borders.

A recent dumpee herself, Julie had been just as confused and vulnerable at the time, and she'd known there would be nothing worse for her ego than a rebound relationship. She and Luc were, and always would be, better off as friends.

"Is that a problem?" Luc asked.

She blinked. "Problem?"

"Us kissing. You got an odd look on your face."

Had she? "It's no problem at all," she assured him.

"We'll have to start acting like a married couple," he said. "You'll have to move in with me. But nothing in our relationship will change. We only have to make it look as if it has."

But by pretending, by making it look real to everyone else, wasn't that in itself a change to their relationship?

Ugh. She'd never realized how complicated this would be.

"Look," he said, frowning. "I want you to stay in the US, but if it's going to cause a rift in our friendship… Do you think it's worth it?"

"It is worth it. And I don't want you to think that I'm not grateful. I am."

"I know you are." He smiled and laid a hand on her forearm, and the feel of his skin against hers gave her that little shiver again.

What the heck was going on between them?

HDEXP0215

HARLEQUIN®
TM
A Romance FOR EVERY MOOD™

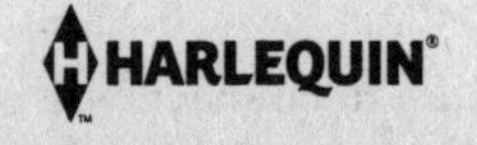

HARLEQUIN®
A Romance FOR EVERY MOOD™